Total-E-Bound Publishing books by Nichelle Gregory:

Djinn Brotherhood
As You Wish
As You Desire

Lovin' Leela
Hearts & Diamonds
Doll
Taken By Surprise

I0542095

AMPLE DELIGHTS

NICHELLE GREGORY

Ample Delights
ISBN # 978-1-78184-548-6
©Copyright Nichelle Gregory 2012
Cover Art by Posh Gosh ©Copyright August 2012
Interior text design by Claire Siemaszkiewicz
Total-E-Bound Publishing

Published in 2012 by Total-E-Bound Publishing, Think Tank, Ruston Way, Lincoln, LN6 7FL, United Kingdom.

Total-E-Bound Publishing is an imprint of Total-E-Ntwined Limited.

AMPLE DELIGHTS

Dedication

Dedicated to my Aunt Neicy, who read this story and many others before they were ever published. Your support and love have helped get me through some dark moments. Thank you for always believing in my work...for telling me to embrace my curves and rock 'em.
I love you!

Dedicated to my husband, who has always treasured my ample delights...
I love you so much!

Dedicated to my sister, who has encouraged and helped me every step of the way...
I love you!

And finally...this book is dedicated to YOU...yes, you, with your gorgeous curves and beautiful spirit. Never be timid or afraid to rock whatcha got because... curvilicious is delicious!!

Chapter One

"Terrah, can you add a few more sparkles to Jocelyn's eye makeup?"

"My pleasure. Can you look up for me?" Terrah asked Jocelyn. She ignored the model's bored sigh as she began to apply more blue rhinestones around her eyes.

The blonde bombshell could be a pain to work with, but today she was worse than usual.

Biting back a sigh of her own, Terrah dusted her brush on her hand before applying more of the smoky bronze eyeshadow to highlight Jocelyn's blue eyes.

"How's this?" Terrah asked, turning to Michelle.

The art director had been instrumental in helping Terrah build her portfolio when she'd first started by recommending her to other clients. Terrah had snagged some of the best jobs of her career because of Michelle's confidence in and praise for her work.

"Perfect!" Michelle looked at her watch. "We start shooting in twenty minutes."

"Perfect," Jocelyn muttered as she scrutinised her appearance in the mirror. She got up from her chair, stunning in the couture evening gown that clung to her slender form, and walked away.

Michelle frowned. "She's in a mood today."

"I couldn't tell."

Her sarcasm wasn't lost on the art director, and they both chuckled as Terrah stored her brushes.

"You'd think she'd be in a great mood" — Michelle shook her head as she fiddled with her iPad — "especially since she's working with Nick today."

Nick Tasso.

Everyone in the world of fashion knew his name. He was one of the most sought-after male models in the business. Tabloid pictures of Nick and Jocelyn kissing in a club had circulated in entertainment news for months. Today would be Terrah's first time working with him.

"Speak of the *gorgeous* devil..."

Terrah glanced up from her makeup case to see Nick approaching them. Her heart skipped a beat as her gaze skated over the Greek model.

Lawd, have mercy.

Nick Tasso was beyond gorgeous. Dressed in an elegant tux, he was positively lethal to any female with a pulse, and Terrah's was racing. He was sexier in person than on the magazine pages she'd never admit to having stared at before arriving at the studio. His thick, dark brown hair gleamed almost black in the studio. He had beautiful...no, *mesmerising* green eyes framed by long, sooty lashes on a profile the gods had surely chiselled with love, by hand. Terrah loved the way his olive skin contrasted perfectly with the pristine white tuxedo shirt, which he wore open, revealing taut abs beneath. His dark good looks *belonged* on the glossy pages of magazines, to be seen and adored by women all over the world.

Adored and ogled.

Terrah cursed under her breath, annoyed by her thoughts. She was used to working in close proximity with beautiful females and males. It was her job, and not once had she been physically attracted to a model.

Until today.

"Ready for me?" Nick asked, flashing them both a brilliant smile before turning his green eyes on Terrah.

His deep voice reminded her of warm leather, strong and soothing to the senses.

"I am." Terrah patted the chair beside her. "Have a seat here."

"You'll be in good hands with Terrah."

Michelle winked at her as Nick sat down. The art director walked off, and Terrah ignored the flutter of butterflies in her stomach as she fished around in her makeup case for the right powder for Nick. She selected a sponge for application, then pivoted on her heels to find Adonis looking right at her.

And that would be because you're right in his face.

"This won't take long. Can you take off your shirt? I don't want to get makeup on it."

"No problem."

Terrah stepped out of his way as he stood up to shrug out of his tuxedo jacket and shirt. Her pulse quickened as her eyes swept over hard, defined muscles. She met his eyes and knew, finally knew, what it meant to be spellbound by a man.

How could she have thought his eyes were simply green? They were aqua green.

Like the ocean.

Terrah straightened her back, annoyed by the flash of heat running up her neck to her cheeks. She prided herself on being a seasoned professional, unaffected by the plethora of male goodness she often found herself surrounded by. Besides, she refused to mentally moon over a pretty-boy model, especially one dating someone as vapid and annoying as Jocelyn. He was obviously into boring, bone-skinny blondes.

Terrah pressed the sponge to Nick's face and quickly blended the foundation into his skin. It took all of her energy to focus on her task and not the strong line of his jaw or his ripped abs she lightly dusted. She was almost done when Jocelyn rounded the small partition in front of Terrah's workspace.

"Nick, we need to talk."

"Not now, Jocelyn."

Terrah sensed rather than heard the steel in Nick's voice. "It's okay, I'm all done." She stepped away from him, hoping they'd leave her area to have their lovers' quarrel.

"Thank you," Nick said with a warm smile.

"You're welcome."

Terrah returned his grin as he got up, grabbed his jacket and shirt and strode past Jocelyn. She couldn't help watching the two models as they walked out of earshot, speaking in hushed tones. It was clear they were at odds about something from Terrah's vantage point. Jocelyn was pissed off, and Nick seemed unconcerned about whatever was bothering her as Michelle effectively ended their little tête-à-tête by calling the models to their places.

Terrah moved toward the set, feeling the familiar surge of adrenaline rush through her as the photo shoot began. With a critical eye, she looked at her work beneath the bright lights. She admired the breathtaking design of the shimmering magenta gown moulded to Jocelyn's willowy frame. The blonde looked amazing, leaning into Nick's sculpted body with her hand pressed on his smooth chest. This shoot was going to catapult Jocelyn into the supermodel stratosphere.

And I did the makeup.

Terrah grinned. She was pleased with her work and the direction her career was taking. Her smiled faded a little as her gaze wandered over to the photographer, who was busy snapping frame after frame.

Aidan Marks.

He still looked the same, carried himself in the same self-assured manner that had drawn her to him when they'd first met, almost five years ago. She'd been impressed by his drive and talent, unable to resist a dinner date when he'd asked her out. In retrospect, she'd been a little star-struck when the up-and-coming photographer had taken an interest in her. Dinner had led to a weekend spent mostly in bed. Terrah could admit to herself now that she'd been bowled over by the older man's attention. She hadn't allowed her heart to get involved with their little fling, but she hadn't forgotten him, either.

Terrah watched Aidan work, captivated by his ability to get the models to give him the shots he wanted. Learning he was going to be the photographer for the photo shoot had been a surprise. She hadn't known exactly what to say to him when she'd planned to say hello. Thankfully, there hadn't been any time to approach him beforehand and she hadn't seen him on the set when she'd been doing the makeup. Terrah was certain he'd long forgotten about their little tryst that had taken place many years ago.

Since then he'd become one of the most critically acclaimed photographers in the business, jet-setting all over the world, working with the most promising models. Whether he remembered Terrah or not, landing her current job with him was a huge accomplishment. Just adding his name to her list of clients was going to open even more doors for her in the future.

She'd been in the business eight years, and it hadn't been an easy road to get to the level she was now. The constant rejections, criticisms and the effort needed to continually prove she was the best at her craft had forced her to grow a thick skin. She took pride in every modelling gig she acquired, maintained her cool in the craziest and most stressful environments and had earned a solid professional reputation.

Her line of work required self-confidence, stamina and the patience of Job. The hours were ridiculously long, the clients could be just as outrageous, and being around beautiful, stick-thin models day in and day out tested one's insecurities daily. But Terrah knew the modelling world inside and out. She saw the models refusing to eat anything but rabbit food, and those were the *sane* diets. The standards for models became more demanding every year, and many stressed over staying on top by being the thinnest. Terrah had witnessed the meltdowns of fatigued models and knew how isolating being in the business could be for many of the girls.

Most people didn't have a clue about all the insanity behind the perfect pictures presented to the mass media. Modelling could be a cut-throat, sometimes *ugly* business, but Terrah respected the process and the people involved.

"*You* did an amazing job! I love the colours you used."

Terrah turned to Ginny, a production assistant she'd worked with before, and smiled. "Thanks. I think the colours I chose complement Jocelyn's dress perfectly."

Ginny nodded, staring at the models. "She looks incredible and I *love* that gown. I'd have to eat nothing but celery sticks for six months to make that swathe of material look good."

Terrah watched Ginny bite into a celery stick. She hated celery. Even the smell of it bothered her.

"Want some?"

Ginny offered her a plastic baggie filled with the one vegetable Terrah couldn't stomach.

"No, thanks."

"What does that chick eat? She's so freakin' thin."

Terrah shrugged. She'd learned to be comfortable with her own body, which wasn't always easy, especially being a size twelve around single digit-wearing females. Her voluptuous curves stood out all the time on set, in a sea of skinny models.

But skinny didn't mean happy.

She couldn't count how many times she'd listened to a size zero waif lamenting about her body. Body image reigned supreme in the lives of the women and men she helped look even more flawless, and Terrah often wondered if the price of perfection was too high. She understood perfection didn't exist, and yet it was her job to help make damn sure it appeared to.

"God, he's hot," Ginny said wistfully as she continued to munch. She looked at Terrah when she didn't respond. "Don't you think Nick Tasso is hot?"

"Like fire."

Ginny snickered as Terrah stared ahead.

Nick commanded the camera. He knew exactly which way to angle his face and body. Terrah stared at Jocelyn and Nick posing. Both of them looked flawless, happy—in love, even, despite what she'd seen transpire between them earlier—as Aidan captured their every move on film. Anyone looking at the supermodels now would believe in the magic of romance. For a fleeting moment, Terrah wished she were still a believer.

* * * *

Nick gritted his teeth as Jocelyn continued to whine. He wanted to keep things civil between them, but she was trying his patience. The photo shoot was over and he was ready to get out from underneath the bright lights.

"I'd hoped you'd call me when you got back to New York."

"I thought we both agreed that night was just that. *One* night."

"We did agree, but... I..."

Usually the perfect picture of confidence, Jocelyn now seemed unsure of herself as she fumbled with her words.

"I thought maybe we could have dinner together?"

"Jocelyn, that's not a good idea."

Nick took one look at the disappointment in Jocelyn's eyes and regretted sleeping with her all over again. An evening out with her and some other models over a month ago had led to drinks, a serious lapse in judgement and the flirtatious blonde ending up in his hotel room.

"Why? What's wrong with having dinner with a friend?"

She was pushing it with the whole 'friend' thing. They worked together well, but they were far from what Nick called friends. The thought of eating with

Jocelyn…correction—of *him* eating while she picked over her food—was totally unappealing. They had nothing to talk about besides modelling and he didn't want to talk shop over a meal. As far as he was concerned they had nothing in common and not an ounce of real chemistry. Even their brief sexual encounter, at least for Nick, had been boring.

Jocelyn just wasn't his type. When he held a woman in his arms he wanted to feel more than bones. He was drawn to women with hourglass figures…full breasts, small waists, hips he could grip and juicy, spankable asses…like the sexy makeup artist with the smooth cocoa skin and the luscious curves.

Terrah.

He'd heard one of the guys on the production crew say her name.

"Nick?"

"What was that?"

He took off his tux jacket as he focused his attention back on Jocelyn.

"What do you think?"

"Think about…?"

"Dinner?"

"Dinner's not going to work for me."

Jocelyn blinked as she frowned, obviously surprised by his response.

"Look, I'm jet-lagged and I'm ready to get out of this tux."

"Sure, okay." Jocelyn averted her eyes from his.

"Great. Are we good?"

She flicked him one of her cool stares and nodded. "Of course. I'm sure I'll see you around. Goodnight."

"'Night," Nick said as Jocelyn walked past him. He blew out a breath before he exited the stage to change.

That had been awkward as hell.

He scanned the studio for Terrah and spotted her in the back by the makeup chair. She stood out, looking vibrant and sexy in the yellow dress she was wearing. The lemon chiffon hue complemented her gorgeous brown skin. An Empire-style bodice accentuated her full breasts while also highlighting her small waistline and the womanly curve of her hips.

Terrah was his type, all day and all night long.

He wanted to put his hands all over her body. Nick's gaze fell on her strappy sandals and he scoped the shapely line of her legs as she bent over to pick up a makeup sponge off the floor. His cock stirred at the sight of her rounded bottom outlined in the dress. The seductive sway and rhythm of her hips and ass mesmerised him as she started to walk towards the door.

Nick picked up his pace.

No way was he letting her leave the building without asking her out first.

Chapter Two

Terrah waved goodbye to Ginny and sighed as she walked towards the door. She was tired and…

Sexually frustrated.

There. Admitting it was half the problem.

Seeking a solution that didn't involve batteries was a whole other ball game.

Why was finding a sensual, romantic, attractive, intelligent man so hard? In her dating experience, they had one or two of those qualities, but not the whole enchilada.

Her last relationship had lasted almost two years, but she'd known that special *something* had been missing. She wanted to feel that spark…that excitement she always fantasised about.

Did such passion and romance exist in real life?

Terrah thought about Nick and Jocelyn posing in front of the elaborate city backdrop, the perfect picture of romance. They'd made a striking couple together. The photos Aidan had taken had been smokin' hot…some of the sexiest she'd seen in a while.

Nick Tasso was the ultimate sexual fantasy.

Terrah wondered if he actually lived up to what he portrayed. She straightened her back and pushed her wayward thoughts out of her mind. It was time for lunch, dinner... When had she last eaten? She couldn't wait to take off her heels, pour a nice glass of red and dig into a hot plate of leftover lasagne. After a warm shower, she'd spend a little time with her insatiable lover.

So what if he was made of silicone? He always got the job done.

"Terrah, wait!"

Damn it.

Terrah halted in her tracks, turning to see Michelle rushing toward her.

"I'm glad I caught you before you left. You did another fabulous job today with Jocelyn's makeup."

Terrah smiled. "Thanks. It's never hard to help Jocelyn look amazing."

"She looked incredible. One would never guess she could be such a brat. I told you this before, but I appreciate how you work around whatever 'tude you're faced with." Michelle touched her arm. "I've got some exciting news!"

"Do tell."

"Aidan Marks would like to use *you* for his upcoming photo shoot in *Hawaii*!"

Terrah blinked in surprise. "Really?"

"Really—he wants to talk with you."

Terrah looked over the art director's shoulder to find Aidan's eyes on her. He smiled at her...the kind of smile that told her he remembered exactly who she was, after all.

"Okay."

Michelle frowned. "Okay? I thought you'd be jumping for joy. This is huge. Aidan Marks personally asked me if you'd like to be the makeup artist for this project!"

"This *is* huge." Terrah laughed. "I'm just shocked. Trust me, I'm *very* excited."

"It is exciting! I wanted to be the one to tell you, since I'll be the art director for the shoot."

"Congratulations."

Michelle grinned, lifting her vibrating cell phone. "To you, too. I'll call you tomorrow with all the details."

"Sounds good."

Terrah resisted the urge to let out a whoop of joy as the art director walked away. She took a deep breath instead and made her way over to where Aidan was talking. It looked like she would be indulging in *two* glasses of wine to celebrate Michelle's news tonight. In fact, she would call her girls and see if they wanted to join her in a special toast, but first she wanted to personally thank Aidan.

The studio had cleared out a little, but there was still a lot of activity going on around her and Aidan stood in the centre of it all. He was an attractive man in his own right, commanding attention with his loud voice and charismatic personality. Long, ebony dreads brushed against his broad shoulders in stark contrast to the yellow button-down shirt he was wearing. Dark jeans and dress shoes gave him a casual yet classy air.

Terrah approached him, refusing to acknowledge the butterflies scattering in her stomach as his attention shifted to her.

"Terrah"—Aidan embraced her with a broad smile—"it's been a long time."

"It has…almost five years." She pulled away, noticing he still wore the same cologne.

"You look even more beautiful than I remember."

"Thank you." She grinned as his gaze swept over her. "You've made quite a career for yourself, Aidan."

"I guess all the hard work is finally paying off. I wondered if it ever would." Aidan took a sip of water from the bottle in his hand. "I think it's paying off for you, as well. I've heard your name in ever-widening circles."

Terrah laughed "Well, I wanted to thank you for the invitation to work with you in Hawaii."

"Of course." Aidan's gaze fell to her lips. "I always thought you did fantastic work. I can't wait to see what you do on the Big Island."

"I won't disappoint you."

Aidan nodded. "I know you won't. I wouldn't have asked for you if I thought you would. So, you won't feel awkward working with me…given our history?"

Heat flamed her cheeks at the mention of their past. "Aidan, that was years ago… Over and forgotten."

"Forgotten?"

Aidan lifted an eyebrow in her direction.

"Forgotten," Terrah repeated. She could see the challenge in Aidan's eyes as his gaze ran over her dress.

"Well, *I* remember every detail."

Stunned, Terrah opened her mouth to respond just as Michelle joined them.

"Aidan, do you still want to discuss the specifics for our upcoming shoot?"

Aidan tore his eyes off Terrah to look at Michelle. "Yes, let's do that now. See you soon, Terrah." He flashed her a meaningful glance. "I'm glad our paths crossed again."

Terrah avoided Michelle's gaze as the photographer leant forward to kiss her on the cheek.

"Let's have dinner together," Aidan whispered in her ear.

He winked at her as he strode off with Michelle, who flicked her a quizzical look.

Dinner with Aidan?

They'd shared some fun times together, but that had been a long time ago. She wasn't interested in striking anything romantic up with him again. Aidan loved Aidan. There was no chance of any of his relationships being about anything other than sex. And she certainly wasn't looking to jump back into bed with him, even though he'd been a good lover. He probably had no idea how much he'd helped her figure out what to look out for in pseudo-relationships.

Terrah sighed.

She'd have to think of a tactful way to get out of going to dinner with Aidan. She knew turning down the world-famous photographer would not go over well. Terrah groaned as she glanced around the practically deserted set. Her gaze unconsciously sought out Nick Tasso. He and Jocelyn were no longer standing by the backdrop. Only a few members of the production and lighting crew remained.

Terrah started walking towards the exit to the studio. She'd worry about Aidan's intentions behind his dinner invitation later. Right now, it was time to go home and celebrate.

All things considered, it had turned out to be a pretty good day.

* * * *

Nick pulled on his T-shirt as he walked down the hall. He'd exited from the studio to strip out of his clothes in one of the fastest wardrobe changes ever when Terrah had stopped to chat with Michelle. Ginny had been thrilled to answer his question about Terrah's whereabouts, and he knew she hadn't left the building yet.

So where was she?

He went past two offices before he found her snagging a bottle of water from the vending machine with one hand as she texted with the other.

"Hello, Terrah."

She whipped around at the sound of his voice, and Nick rushed forward as she lost her balance and fumbled to keep hold of her phone. Neither of them could save the device from hitting the floor with a loud clatter beside her makeup case.

"Damn."

They both leant down to pick up the phone and bumped heads instead.

"Ouch!"

"I'm so sorry."

He handed the cell phone to her with an apologetic grin as they both straightened up.

Smooth, Tasso, real smooth.

"Is it broken?"

Terrah pushed buttons on the phone. "The screen isn't lighting up as it should."

His gaze swept over her lovely, heart-shaped face and fell to her mouth as she continued to fiddle with her cell. She had the most incredible pair of lips he'd ever seen.

Those lips are made for kisses.

Nick pushed back the errant thought as Terrah softly cursed.

"I didn't mean to startle you. If your phone is broken, I'll replace it."

Her fingers stopped flying over her cell and her cinnamon-brown eyes met his.

"It was an accident, no worries. I've dropped it before and it's come back to life. It could be fine in a few hours and, if not, it was time for me to get a new one anyway."

"Are you sure?"

Terrah grinned. "Positive. Were you looking for Jocelyn? I think I saw her just getting ready to go."

"No, actually, I was looking for you."

The surprise on her face quickly changed to a look of concern.

"Is it the makeup? Did you have an allergic reaction?"

Her gaze flicked over his face and chest before she lifted her eyes to his. The concern he saw in her beautiful brown eyes stirred him.

And her lips…

Just watching those full, totally kissable lips move with each spoken word was beginning to give him a hard-on.

"I'm not here about the makeup."

His gaze ran appreciatively over Terrah's hair. He wanted to touch one of the dark curls she'd restrained in a low ponytail. She tilted her head and his eyes were drawn to the dainty silver earrings swaying in her earlobes.

"No?"

The quizzical look on her face made him smile.

"No. I wanted to invite you to dinner."

"Dinner?"

Terrah's eyes widened as he took a step closer.

"Yes. Let me take you to dinner, especially since I'm the reason you dropped your phone."

"That's really not necessary." Her gaze narrowed as she stared at him. She shifted her eyes from his to mess with her cell again."Besides, I don't go to dinner with involved men."

"Involved?"

"Yes, *involved*." Terrah shook her head as she unscrewed the cap on her water. "Does Jocelyn know you're in here trying to hit on me?"

"I'm not involved with Jocelyn."

One sculpted eyebrow lifted in his direction.

"Oh, really?"

"Really."

"Well, not according to the tabloids."

"Haven't you heard the phrase, 'Don't believe everything you read'?"

Terrah scoffed. "Okay, so you're not *involved* with Jocelyn…just *sleeping* with her. I get it."

"No, I don't think you do."

Nick studied her as she took a sip of water. His eyes dipped to her mouth again and he wondered how such delectable lips could utter such sassy words. He frowned as Terrah let out a resigned sigh and waved her hand.

"Have a good night, Nick."

* * * *

Terrah brushed past Nick, utterly confused by the mixture of excitement and contempt making her heart pound. She still couldn't believe he'd asked her out.

The nerve of some men.

Nick Tasso was a player, obviously not accustomed to having his dinner invitations turned down. Terrah walked faster and her heels echoed loudly in the hallway. She reached the exit, pushed through the door and took a deep breath as she stepped outside. The sun had not yet set, and the sidewalk was filled with busy New Yorkers hurrying to get home in the summer heat.

Terrah joined them, taking her MP3 player out of her shoulder bag and walking towards the subway. Nick's invitation to dinner had shocked the hell out of her, completely thrown her for a loop. For the briefest of moments, she had been thrilled, blindsided by his ridiculously intoxicating good looks. Thank goodness she'd come to her senses. She hadn't even been tempted to say yes.

Right.

Terrah boarded the subway, grateful to find a window seat. She sat down, turned up Adele's song of love and loss, surprised by the sting of tears in her eyes. She swallowed them down, changed to a more upbeat tune and froze in her seat.

Her makeup case!

She'd been so distracted by Nick's proposal, she'd left it in the room by the vending machine.

Damn!

Incensed, Terrah got up from her seat to get off at the next stop. Her makeup supply had cost her a fortune. Plus, she had colours of lipstick and eyeshadow that were irreplaceable. As much as she didn't want to, she had to go back.

The sun was slipping from the sky by the time she made her way out of the subway and back to the studio. She pushed the buzzer and yanked the door open as the lock was released. The sound of familiar laughter behind her drew her attention. She turned just in time to see Jocelyn get into a shiny Mercedes parked alongside the kerb, with another male model Terrah had worked with before. Terrah watched the two of them exchange a hot kiss before Jocelyn's man for the night pulled the car into traffic and it sped off.

Maybe Nick had told her the truth about his and Jocelyn's relationship status.

What does it matter?

Weary, Terrah walked back down the hallway towards the room where she hoped her case still was. She stepped inside the doorway and cursed out loud.

Her makeup was gone.

"Looking for this?"

Terrah spun around to see her beloved case in Nick's upheld hand. "Omigoodness, yes!" Her heart skipped a beat as her gaze locked with his. "Thank you."

"You're welcome."

Why did his deep voice send shivers of delight up her spine?

"I thought someone had taken it."

Terrah tried to appear cool when she was anything but after rushing back off the subway to get her stuff. She was hot and flustered to find herself face to face with Nick again.

"I picked it up right after you stormed out of here."

"Thanks again—" Terrah glared at him. "Stormed?"

Chapter Three

"*Stormed.*" Nick emphasised the word as Terrah fiddled with her shoulder bag.

"Can you just give me my case, please? It's been a really long day. I'm so tired and hungry…" Terrah shot him a quick look. "That was not an invitation to *extend* another invitation."

Nick chuckled. "I didn't assume it was…but my invitation still stands."

He handed her the case, struck again by how lovely she was. She had the most expressive eyes and it wasn't hard for him to see the wariness in her level gaze.

"Before you say no for the second time, I'd like to say again that I am not involved with Jocelyn…or anyone, for that matter. It would make my night if you changed your mind and said yes. Are you really going to say no to sharing a meal with the man who stayed around to guard your makeup?"

Terrah laughed, and the girlish sound of it made Nick smile.

"Fine. We'll go to dinner. It'll save me from having to wash dishes later."

"Great. Let's go."

He couldn't remember the last time he'd had to work so damn hard to convince a woman to go out with him.

Eating with him would save her from doing dishes? *Damn.*

The woman was seriously trying to bruise his ego.

Terrah lifted her face to his as he held open the door for her with a hesitant smile. His eyes were drawn once again to the tempting fullness of her lips as they curved upward, and that was when he saw it. That tiny flicker of desire flashing in her eyes before she masked it.

She was attracted to him.

It was on.

Nick resisted the unexpected urge to sweep her into his arms as she stepped by him and onto the sidewalk. He could almost envision what it would feel like to kiss her. He'd start off slow, run his tongue along the generous swell of her bottom lip. He wanted to make her wet and hungry for more. He would not stop pursuing her until she craved *him*.

"What do you have a taste for?" Nick asked after he cleared his throat.

"I could go for anything right now."

Her innocent statement sent all kinds of erotic images through his head, of the two of them intertwined beneath his sheets. His body overreacted against his will and Nick stuffed one hand into his jeans, hoping to camouflage his semi-erect cock as they walked.

"All right, I know a great restaurant on Madison Avenue. Do you want to just catch a cab?"

"Yes! I didn't wear my comfortable heels."

Nick glanced down at her shoes, thinking her non-comfy shoes showcased her killer legs well.

Terrah pulled on the strap of her shoulder bag. "I wish I could drop off my gear before we go to dinner."

"I'm staying in a hotel not far from the restaurant I'd like to take you to. We could drop your stuff off there, if you'd like?" Nick saw the suspicion in her eyes. "We could just leave it at the front desk. You could swing by and grab your case afterwards."

"Well…"

"C'mon, Terrah, I'm not propositioning you for sex."

He grabbed her arm as she stumbled.

"I didn't say you were."

"Your eyes, Terrah… Your eyes say it for you. Let me have this stuff."

Nick stopped in the middle of the sidewalk and Terrah followed suit. He slipped his fingers beneath the strap of her shoulder bag, pulled it off her shoulder, placed it on his own and took the makeup case back from her hand.

"So what's it going to be? Do you want to lug your gear with us or drop it off?" Nick asked as he hailed a cab.

"Drop it off."

"Good."

Nick stepped to the kerb as a yellow taxi pulled up and Terrah moved beside him. He opened her door and wondered what kind of perfume she wore. The damnable sexy scent wafted into his nose and lingered as she got into the car. Nick envisioned what it would be like to kiss Terrah's thighs as she slid back into her seat and unknowingly offered him a tempting peek. His cock, which had finally decided to behave, stirred at the thought when he slammed her door closed.

Keep thinking like that and you won't be able to hide your hard-on.

Nick went around the other side of the cab, got in and closed his own door. After giving the address for his hotel to the cabbie, he turned to Terrah just as the first few bars of Jamie Foxx's *Unpredictable* began to chime.

Terrah started to chuckle as she took her cell out of her purse, checked the display and silenced it.

"What is so funny?"

"This song is so fitting for this moment." Terrah shook her head as she looked at him. "Going out to dinner with you is the *last* thing I expected tonight... Completely unpredictable."

"Hey, I'm glad I get to spare you a night of having to wash dishes."

Terrah laughed. "You're funny."

Nick grinned at her as the taxi wove in and out of traffic. Terrah didn't know it yet, but the joke was about to be on her. He could tell she thought she had his type pegged, but he was going to show her just how unpredictable he was.

* * * *

Terrah took Nick's hand as he opened her door, and got out of the cab. She tried to ignore the way her pulse reacted as he smiled at her.

Why did he have to be so charming on top of gorgeous?

"It's not so hot now," Nick said as they walked up to his hotel.

"Thank goodness."

It *was* cooler now the sun had set, but the air was still muggy. She didn't like the heat, but New York weather was the last thing on her mind. Underneath the calm façade she was trying hard to keep in place, she was freaking out.

She was going to dinner with Nick Tasso, her ultimate fantasy guy. It was crazy. She shouldn't have accepted his second invitation to dinner, but she hadn't been able to say no. Not with him waiting for her to accept with those sexy, hypnotic, green eyes of his. Besides, he'd earned a dinner date for sticking around with her makeup case. She appreciated what he'd done no matter what his motives had been.

Terrah flicked a glance at Nick and decided she wasn't going to focus on *why* he'd asked her out right now. He appeared to be oblivious to the attention he was garnering from just about everyone they passed by. She wasn't unaccustomed to men looking at her, but this was something else. Nick was getting play from males and females, and he seemed completely unaware of it all.

Duh, he's a top model.

Being constantly stared at was the status quo for him.

And he truly was something to stare at.

The sky-blue T-shirt he was wearing highlighted his bronze skin and muscled arms. He pulled open the glass door in front of them, and Terrah couldn't help noticing the smattering of dark hairs running up his forearms. A much-needed blast of cold air rushed over her heated skin as they stepped into the opulent lobby.

"Your agency put you up in style, I see."

Nick laughed. "I rent one of the penthouse suites here."

"Oh."

Of course he did.

"Nice. I've never been in this hotel."

"You should see the view from my bedroom."

Bedroom.

Terrah picked up her pace to keep up with Nick's long-legged strides, disturbed that she couldn't imagine anything else in his bedroom but him…beckoning to her to join him on the crisp white sheets.

She swallowed hard, distracted by her naughty thoughts as they stopped at the front desk. Her mind continued to race while she absently listened to him talk to the concierge. Nick was fine as hell, so she was allowed a moment of pure lust.

She was having a totally normal female reaction to being in the proximity of a major hottie.

"Terrah?"

Terrah blinked and heat rushed to her cheeks. "I'm sorry, what did you just say?"

"They're going to hold your case and bag here until we get back from dinner."

"Perfect." Terrah smiled at the hotel clerk as Nick placed her stuff on the shiny front desk. "Thank you."

The hotel clerk smiled. "Not a problem. Just give Melanie the ticket I gave you when you return, Mr Tasso."

"Thank you."

Terrah sucked in a breath as Nick took hold of her arm and guided her past a group of tourists. White-hot waves of awareness rippled over her in reaction to his warm hand on her skin. She was relieved when he dropped his hold on her.

"We're just one block away from one of the best restaurants in New York," Nick said as they crossed through the lobby.

"Can't be if I've never been to it."

"You've never been to—?"

Terrah yelped as someone collided with her and stepped on her foot.

"Sorry," the starry-eyed teen said, barely glancing Terrah's way as she stared up at Nick. "OMG! You're that underwear model in *GQ*!"

Nick smiled graciously as he nodded. "I am."

"Oh, wow! I can't believe I just bumped into you!"

Bumped into me, *you mean.* Terrah bit her tongue to keep from correcting the jubilant brunette, who pulled out a camera phone.

"Can I please have a picture?"

"Of course," Nick said, stepping up beside the blushing teenager, who held out her phone to Terrah.

"Would you take our picture?"

Nick winked at her over the teen's head.

"Sure."

Never mind my crushed toes.

Terrah forced a smile, knowing she wasn't being fair. Hadn't she just had an 'oh, my God' moment herself?

"On the count of three… One, two, three."

The brunette squealed with delight as she took her cell from Terrah and focused her attention back on Nick.

"Would you sign my purse?"

"Your purse?" Nick asked, looking down at the girl's designer bag.

Terrah wondered if it was possible for the chick to turn any redder.

"Yes, please!"

"Well, okay."

The brunette began frantically digging through her purse, then offered Nick a marker with a wide smile. Terrah guessed the girl to be about sixteen years old.

"There you go," Nick said, handing the teenager back her freshly autographed bag.

"Thank you so much! I'm such a huge fan of your work. My friends are going to be *so* sorry they didn't go shopping with me today."

"It was my pleasure."

Nick gave the female a quick hug, sending her off into another tizzy of squeals as they walked through the hotel lobby to the main entrance.

"You just made her entire year, I bet."

Terrah thanked the doorman as they stepped outside.

"She was sweet. I'm just glad we got away out there before anyone else recognised me. I always take the time to chat or sign autographs for fans, but there are times when I'd rather not get caught up in the hoopla that goes along with this business."

"Really?"

Terrah could just imagine the party invites and the women willing and ready to do anything to get Nick to notice them.

"C'mon, you can't think signing autographs and taking pictures when you're just going out for coffee or groceries would be fun *all* the time."

"No, I guess not, but you were very gracious."

"I'm always gracious."

He winked at her, making Terrah smile, while opening the restaurant door for her. She took in the stylish décor and intimate dining atmosphere as the hostess greeted them.

"Your table is ready, Mr Tasso."

They were led to a secluded table and the hostess waited for them both to take their seats before offering menus. Terrah's gaze was drawn to the pink gerbera daisies in a crystal vase before her. The rich colour of the petals stood out on the elegant, white linen tablecloth. The wine glasses sparkled and the silverware gleamed in the subtle lighting. This was definitely not the kind of restaurant you could just walk into and get a table.

"Did you call ahead?" Terrah asked, shifting her gaze to Nick.

"I know the owner and I'm a regular customer when I'm in the city."

Terrah nodded, liking his modesty. He could've just said, 'I've got it like that.' She'd been around models who loved to boast about their abilities to get into certain places wherever and whenever they wanted.

"Mmm…it smells delicious in here."

"Wait until you taste their marinated lamb. Do you like Mediterranean food?"

"I can't say I've tried a lot of different dishes, but I do like hummus."

Nick smiled. "There's a lot more to Mediterranean food than hummus, but that's a good place to start. The hummus here tastes almost as good as the one my mother makes. Are you comfortable with me ordering some dishes for you to try?"

His eyes seemed to darken as he waited for her response, and Terrah's pulse sped up another notch.

It's just the fancy lighting.

"Sure, but only if I get to pick the wine."

"Be my guest. Here's the wine list."

Terrah took the smaller menu from his hand, grateful for something else to look at besides those aqua-green eyes. The feel of his gaze on her was equivalent to the heat of the sun in the middle of a New York City heatwave.

Mmm…maybe hotter, Terrah mused, making her wine selection just as their waitress returned to take their order. She was sure it was all practised seduction, but it was working...a little too well.

The waitress batted her eyelashes at Nick while nodding her approval of the dishes he selected. Clearly, she wasn't immune to his sex appeal either.

Hello – what female would be?

"So, tell me, Terrah, why did you get into makeup?"

Nick's leg brushed up against hers beneath the table, and Terrah straightened her back and cleared her throat. She hesitated for a second, contemplating how in-depth her answer should be.

"Long story short, my dad refused to let me wear any until I was, like, sixteen. So, I think I developed a huge obsession for the stuff. I wanted to know about every brand, product, and application out there." Terrah lifted her glass of wine and took a sip. "I decided to build a career around what I love."

"It shows in your work."

His compliment and his sexy grin set off a wildfire in her blood. Terrah shifted in her seat, annoyed by how easy it would be to simply melt under the warmth of Nick's gaze.

"Thank you."

Their gazes locked for a moment before Terrah looked away.

"For a makeup artist, you wear a surprisingly small amount of makeup."

He leaned in to the table, studying her face in earnest, and another embarrassing rush of heat suffused her cheeks.

"You've heard the old adage, 'Less is more.' The average female doesn't require a lot of makeup to look good."

"I tend to agree, but" – his voice dropped to a conspiratorial tone, and Terrah officially melted as he leaned across the table—"there's *nothing* average about you."

Chapter Four

Terrah smiled, trying to ignore the erratic beat of her heart as she wrapped her fingers around her wine glass.

So, Nick was a charmer in front of the camera *and* off.

"I meant the women who aren't in the modelling business."

"I know."

Terrah watched him lift his glass and take a sip of the wine she'd chosen.

"Great choice of wine... One of my favourites, actually. We have the same taste in merlot, it seems."

Terrah traced a circle around the mouth of her glass, aware of Nick's gaze dipping to her lips. She exhaled as butterflies flitted around in her stomach, convinced his eyes could melt steel. To her dismay, the butterflies within her seemed to change into flutters of desire.

Heaven help me.

Miraculously, her phone began to chime in her purse.

"Excuse me," Terrah said to Nick as she reached for her purse, grateful for the distraction.

She took out her cell, saw her sister calling and answered.

"Hey, Audrey."

"Hey, yourself. How'd your shoot go?"

Terrah grinned, happy to hear her sister's voice. Audrey never wasted time with small talk.

"Really well. Can I call you back?"

"What are you doing?"

Terrah glanced at Nick. "About to have dinner."

"With?"

She hesitated to say it, knowing Audrey would never let her off the phone if she answered her question.

"Terrah?"

"I'll call you back."

"Tonight?"

"Yup."

"Bye."

Terrah hung up as their food arrived. "Sorry about that."

"No problem."

"My sister always checks in with me about the same time every day."

Nick served her a piece of lamb. "Does she live here in New York?"

"No, Chicago."

"Just the two of you guys?"

"Yes. What about you?"

"I've got a brother. He lives in California with the rest of my family."

"Are you two close?"

"Very. What about you and your sister?"

"She's my best friend in the whole world. I wish I could see her more often." Terrah grinned, then took a bite. "Oh, wow, this is melt-in-your-mouth good."

"Isn't it? Try that hummus and tell me it's not the best you've ever had."

Terrah moved forward in her chair to dip her flatbread into the creamy spread and winced as her shoe bumped into the pole beneath the table.

"What's wrong?"

"Your teeny-bopper fan stepped on the top of my foot and it kills."

Nick frowned. "You didn't say anything."

Terrah shrugged. "She didn't mean to and it was no big deal." She tasted the hummus, enjoying the savoury flavours bursting on her tongue. "You're right, this *is* the best hummus ever."

"Let me see your foot."

She stopped chewing to stare at him. "What?"

"You heard me. Let me see your foot. I happen to be an expert at foot massage." Nick held her gaze as the waitress poured more wine into their glasses and walked away. "Just lift your leg under the table and I'll make the pain go away."

His words and the tone of his deep voice sent a bolt of sexual awareness through Terrah.

Make the pain go away? He had the power to make her forget her *name*.

"Oh, you're *good*."

"Excuse me?"

He had the nerve to look confused as Terrah wagged her finger at him. "I know what you are trying to do."

"And what's that?"

"Seduce me."

"I was flirting," Nick said without missing a beat.

Something wild twisted in her soul as he held her gaze, placed his elbows on the table and leaned towards her.

"Terrah, I'm not *trying* to seduce you right now, but, if I was, you would know just how *good* I am."

At a loss for words, Terrah averted her eyes from Nick's. She picked up her glass of water and took a sip, hoping to dislodge the huge lump in her throat that affected her breathing.

"Now that we've cleared that up, I'd still like to see your foot."

"It's fine, really."

"Scared?" Nick asked with a deep chuckle.

Terrah lifted her chin as she met his eyes. "Of?"

"Me."

"That's ridiculous. Why would I be scared of you?"

"Not scared of me," Nick said, taking a sip of wine, "scared of the mutual attraction between us."

Mutual attraction?

His words made her heart beat in double time.

The challenge in his eyes compelled her to lift her foot under the table. She had to prove to him, and to herself, that she wasn't scared, because she was beginning to think she had something to fear. The clink of silverware and chatter around them seemed to fade into the background. Nick captured her shoe with one hand, placed her foot on his knee and unbuckled the slim strap. Terrah sucked in a breath as his large hand wrapped around her ankle and he placed the sandal on the floor. His fingers gingerly crested over the top of her foot and her pulse raced. He kept his eyes on her face while touching the slight bump where his fan had injured her.

"I'm so sorry you were hurt."

"It's okay."

It took a considerable amount of control to articulate her sentence with his warm hands gently massaging her entire foot.

Breathe in…breathe out.

Her mental pep talk kept her from removing her foot from his grasp. Nick caressed the knot over the top of her arch and Terrah took another sip from her wine glass to cover her physical reaction to his touch. His palm pressed against the back of her toes as he smiled at her.

"Better?"

"Yes. Thank you."

"You're welcome," Nick said, his thumb stroking the side of her foot.

Nick Tasso is flirting with me.

She couldn't believe she was sitting across the table from one of the sexiest men on the planet, with his hand wrapped around her foot.

He's a player, girl.

Images of Jocelyn in Nick's arms popped into her mind, and Terrah shifted in her seat as Nick bent down, retrieved her wedge sandal and slipped it on her foot. She was certain he knew exactly how his touch was messing up her head.

How could he be attracted to her?

She was as about as different from Jocelyn as night was from day.

* * * *

Nick wondered what was going through Terrah's mind as she moved her fork over the greens on her plate. No way was she immune to the electric vibe between them. He ate an olive and wondered if she was as affected by him touching her as he had been.

"What are you thinking about?"

Terrah finished the bite she'd taken from her salad and pointed towards her plate. "I love the feta cheese mixed in with these greens."

"Yeah, it works well. That's what you were really thinking about?"

Her tongue swept across the full swell of her bottom lip, and Nick followed the movement before meeting her eyes.

"I was thinking about you and Jocelyn."

"Why are you bringing her up?"

"If she's your type…how in the hell can you be attracted to me?"

Nick grinned, appreciating her straight-to-the-point personality. "I am not attracted to Jocelyn."

Nick knew Terrah didn't believe him. He could see the doubt in those huge brown eyes that stared him down.

"Not attracted? She's a *supermodel*."

"And?"

"It looked like attraction in those pictures the whole world saw on television."

"Have you ever slept with someone and regretted it the minute afterwards?"

Nick waited for Terrah to answer his question, wishing he hadn't placed her foot on his leg. All of his blood had begun rushing to his cock the instant he'd started touching her. He wanted to kiss the small bump on her foot.

Hell, I want to kiss her everywhere.

"Well, Terrah, have you ever taken someone to bed and wished you hadn't?"

Nick waited for her answer as she toyed with her fork.

"Of course…*once*."

"That's what happened between Jocelyn and me."

"I get it."

"That's what your lips are saying, but your eyes are telling me something else. I think you've got this preconceived notion about me."

Sooty lashes obscured her eyes from his as she glanced down.

"I don't know you."

"Not yet, but you still think you know what I'm about."

"I think you're a flirt."

Nick chuckled. "I can be."

"I think you're used to women falling all over you."

They both looked at their waitress, who stopped to pour more wine into their glasses.

"Terrah—"

"Thank you again for waiting around with my case. It would've been a pain to replace all of that makeup if it had gone missing."

"No problem. I was going to wait at least twenty minutes for you to come for it. I would've made sure you got it back one way or another."

Terrah glanced at her phone as it chimed. "And it appears my phone is no worse for wear." She fiddled inside her purse and took out her wallet. "Dinner will be my treat—my way of thanking you for safeguarding what I consider valuable."

"Terrah…" He waited for her to look up at him. "Put your wallet away now. I'm glad your cell isn't broken and that you've got your case. I don't want you to pay for dinner and you should know I was going to ask you out before the phone or makeup events happened."

"You were?"

The incredulous look on Terrah's face made him want to kiss her. He was beginning to think that it would be the only way to convince her of his genuine interest.

"You caught my attention from the moment I saw you today. I planned to talk to you after the photo shoot and ask you out."

Nick dropped his gaze from Terrah's wide eyes to her full bottom lip caught between her teeth. "You look surprised."

"I am."

"Why?"

Terrah gave him an impatient look as she finished sampling an olive.

"*Because* you're Nick Tasso, an international supermodel!"

"And?"

Terrah gave him a rueful grin.

"Dinner dates can't be hard for you to come by."

"Charming dinner dates with a beautiful, *interesting* woman are harder to come by than you might think."

"So you find me beautiful and interesting?"

"I do."

"I'm flattered."

"You don't believe me."

Terrah tilted her face with a little smile, and Nick admired her high cheekbones and flawless skin.

"I'm not sure."

"Well, believe me when I tell you that I imagined the two of us sharing a meal like we are right now."

"You did?"

"Why is that so hard for you to believe?"

"It's unexpected. I'd assumed you were attracted to females who look like Jocelyn."

Nick scoffed. "As I said before, I'm not."

Terrah's expression bordered on disbelief. "You're *not* attracted to her? She's gorgeous!"

"She's got nothing on you."

Not a damn thing.

Nick shrugged. "I'm serious."

Seconds ticked by. He stared at Terrah until she broke eye contact.

"You *are* a charmer, aren't you?" She shook her head with a grin as she ate more of her salad.

Nick set down his fork, frustrated by Terrah's dismissive smile. He couldn't remember the last time he'd been shot down by a woman he was genuinely interested in.

"Terrah?"

She glanced up at him with one sculpted eyebrow raised.

"Jocelyn may be gorgeous to every other man in here, but she's not my type...at all."

"I hear you."

"No, I don't think you do."

"Are my eyes giving me away again?"

Nick chuckled. "You think I'd pick her over you if I had to choose?"

"Most men would."

"I think you'd be surprised." Nick's gaze skimmed over Terrah's modest, but no less tempting display of cleavage. "Plus, Jocelyn couldn't ever hope to make that dress look so damn good."

Terrah glanced down at her dress in surprise. "Oh, really?"

The neckline had shifted, plunging downward to reveal a more tempting peek of flesh. Nick waited for her to fix it, but she looked up at him instead.

"Indeed."

Terrah had the kind of body that garnered attention, even though he could see she was more of a conservative dresser. The soft canary hue of her dress popped against her beautiful, honey-brown skin and the fabric melded to her curves...curves he wanted to touch.

"Stop flirting with me."

Nick watched Terrah adjust her dress, taking away his lovely view.

"I don't think I can."

"So I'm the lucky gal tonight, eh?"

"Excuse me?"

She speared a mini tomato with her fork and waved it at him. "I like to celebrate a successful shoot with homemade lasagne and a nice bottle of wine. *You* must like to celebrate with a one-night stand." She rushed on as she set down her fork. "Well, I'm not going to sleep with you—"

"Stop." Nick reached across the table and placed his hand over hers. "Let's get a few things straight, shall we?"

Terrah didn't respond as she lifted her gaze from his hand on top of hers.

"I typically celebrate a successful shoot with a juicy burger and a beer. And Terrah?"

"Hmm..."

She seemed to shiver as she stared at him, and Nick imagined her having that same reaction as he pressed her into the sheets.

"Although it may appear otherwise, there is nothing going on between Jocelyn and me. I'm not attracted to stick-thin models."

Chapter Five

"Okay." Terrah cleared her throat, distracted by the intensity of Nick's gaze as his eyes swept over her body. "You're not attracted to tall, long-legged blondes and you weren't hoping to seduce me into your bed as a way of celebrating a successful shoot. Got it."

Nick laughed. "Good. I'm glad we got that cleared up."

"You must think I'm rude."

"Not at all."

Terrah averted her face as she exhaled. "Well, I've just found it's so much easier to be upfront and direct with people."

"People, or men?"

"Both."

"Understood and respected."

She couldn't focus with him staring at her. He was too much for her senses…beyond gorgeous, funny, easy-going, and a gentleman?

"Should we order dessert?" Nick asked, placing his napkin on the table.

"Mmm…I don't think I can eat anything else."

Terrah watched Nick signal their waitress, aware of other women checking out her dinner companion. She knew he could have a one-night stand every day of the week if he wanted.

The amazing thing about him was he seemed not to care, or even notice, when females threw glances his way. His undivided attention had been hers throughout the entire meal. Terrah observed their waitress fawning over Nick as he requested their check. The brunette hurried off and returned in a flash with the bill, handing it over to him with a flirty smile on her lips.

"Here you go," Nick said, placing his credit card inside the leather pocket. He handed it back with a grin that clearly melted the young woman's heart before turning to Terrah. "So, would you come back here for dinner?"

"Absolutely. I enjoyed the food and the atmosphere."

"What about the company?"

His teasing tone did something weird to her pulse as she nodded.

"Present company included."

Nick opened his mouth to speak, but stopped short as their waitress returned to the table with his credit card and the bill. He quickly signed his name on the slip of paper and gave it back.

Their waitress beamed. "Thank you. I hope you both have a lovely evening."

Terrah and Nick both thanked her before she walked away from their table.

"Nick?"

"Yes?" he asked, slipping his card back into his wallet.

"Thanks again for dinner. This was fun."

"It was my pleasure, Terrah. Shall we?"

Terrah nodded as he stood and came around to the back of her chair. She moved her legs from under the table to stand up and realised her sandal was still unfastened.

"Here—let me."

He moved in front of her, knelt on one knee and proceeded to secure the strap as Terrah tried to ignore the frissons of awareness dancing up her ankle and leg. He stood again, offering his hand, and she took it as he helped her up. Terrah glanced down at their intertwined fingers and a tingle zipped through her. She tried easing her hand from his, but he held on tight, leading them through the restaurant toward the exit. Terrah glanced at Nick, grateful he released his hand from hers as he opened the door for her. They stepped outside the air-conditioned restaurant back into the humid night air, and Terrah shivered as a warm breeze washed over her chilled skin. It was embarrassing how fast her body reacted to his touch.

"Ahh..." Nick nodded. "Now it's the perfect temperature out here. I love summer nights in New York."

"Me too."

"Should we live dangerously and take a taxi back to my hotel for your stuff?"

"It's a gorgeous night for walking, but my feet would want me to say yes. Let's live dangerously!"

Nick smiled. "We wouldn't want to disappoint your feet."

Terrah couldn't help appreciating his muscled arm while he raised his hand and signalled an approaching taxi. He had oodles of sex appeal and the charm to go with it, and Terrah wished she could say she was immune.

But you're not.

Her gaze ran over the slight bulge in the front of his jeans as he stuffed one hand into his pocket and opened the door of the cab for her. She slid into the seat and pulled the door closed as Nick got in on the other side. Her eyes dropped to his hard thighs, showcased nicely in his dark denim jeans. He seemed crowded in the back seat, his long legs bumping into hers as the taxi took off and merged into traffic. Another quick manoeuvre by the taxi driver sent her slamming against Nick.

She sucked in a breath as he shot out a hand to touch her knee. "Maybe we should've walked."

Nick chuckled. "I've travelled around the world, but I always look forward to the wild cab rides when I'm back in the Big Apple."

The only *wild* thing happening to Terrah was the curious heat skittering up her knee and thigh from Nick's touch. It took all of her concentration to respond at the appropriate times as he asked her questions about her work and upcoming projects. She inwardly breathed a sigh of relief when the cab finally came to a stop.

"Here we are."

Her evening out of the *Twilight Zone* was about to come to an end. Nick opened her door and Terrah took his hand. She stepped out of the taxi, feeling a little disappointed. Despite her reservations, she'd enjoyed her dinner with Nick.

She picked up her pace and smiled at the doorman who held open the door for them. The hotel was teeming with activity. She could hear soft jazz music over people talking and relaxing in the deep-seated couches in the lobby area. Terrah followed Nick to the front desk and was once again reminded of his celebrity status. She lost track of the number of women who gave him a second or third look as they passed by.

Hey, ladies! He's not only gorgeous, but intelligent, funny and charming.

"Here you go." Nick handed over her favourite carry-all shoulder bag.

"Thank you."

She lifted her bag up over her head and onto her shoulder before reaching for her case on the counter.

Time to say goodbye. Do it first.

Terrah lifted her face to his. "Well, Nick—"

"I want to show you something before you go. Come with me?"

Terrah stared at him, wondering if he was about to prove her right after all.

He flashed a megawatt grin, as if he could read her mind. "It's here on the main floor."

How could she say no? "Okay."

Nick took her free hand and guided her across the lobby into the hall. They passed two banquet rooms before he stepped inside an arched doorway. He led them past a darkened room, where the only source of light emanated from the gigantic aquarium set into the wall.

"Oh, wow!"

Nick nodded. "I couldn't let you leave without seeing one of this hotel's best features."

"It's incredible."

Terrah stared at the tropical fish flitting about the lush aquatic setting, complete with a sunken ship and a mermaid singing bubbles. She stepped up to the huge tank, set her case down and leaned into the glass for a closer look as Nick came to stand beside her.

"That blue tang is so pretty!" Terrah turned towards Nick, noticing the empty lounge chairs behind them. "This would be a great spot for a small party."

"Or a private dinner."

Images of the two of them dining alone in the beautiful room instantly popped into her head.

Why couldn't she have this kind of sexual chemistry on an actual date?

"Thanks for showing me this." She gestured towards the tank. "I had a great time tonight."

"Does that surprise you, Terrah?"

"A little bit."

Nick shook his head. "You're doing a real number on my ego."

Terrah laughed. "I'm sorry."

"No, you're not."

Ripples of heat spun deep inside her and rushed through every pore of her body as he held her gaze.

Keep it cool.

"Maybe we'll get to work together again on a photo shoot in the near future."

Her heart skipped a beat as Nick grinned. Not his regular curve of the lips—no, the slow, sexy, 'I'm one hundred per cent male' smile.

"Maybe."

Terrah's heart beat erratically as seconds ticked by. Nervous, she glanced back at the aquarium. If she got any hotter she'd break into a sweat.

"Terrah?"

"Yes?"

She turned to him and her breath hitched when she saw the searing look in his eyes.

Omigod—

One arm snaked around her so fast she could only react by placing her hands on his shoulders as she lifted her face to his. Strong fingers gripped her chin and her heart stopped beating in the split second it took for his mouth to descend on hers. She moaned deep in her throat as she parted her lips for him. Nick kissed her slowly, taking time to taste her tongue, melding his mouth with hers. He released her chin and pulled her closer to him as he wrapped his other arm around her waist. Terrah kissed him back, helpless to do anything but respond to her attraction to him and his incredible lip work.

Breathless, she blinked in confusion when he broke the erotic kiss.

"Was that for your ego?"

Terrah marvelled at how steady her voice was. Inwardly, she was quaking in a million molten pieces.

"Don't," Nick said against her temple.

"Don't what?"

She was regaining her sanity with each passing second. All she had to do was get out of his arms and she'd be back in control.

Nick pulled back, but didn't let her go as he looked down at her. "Don't act like you weren't affected by my kiss." His thumb brushed her bottom lip and Terrah trembled. "You don't have to admit it...*this* time."

"There won't be a second time."

Nick only chuckled and the husky sound, coupled with the scent of his cologne, was like a potent aphrodisiac to her system.

"I love your lips."

The timbre of his voice was deeper, huskier...sexier.

"I had to kiss you. I hope you aren't offended."

Offended?

She was on fire, burning for more kisses, more *everything*.

"Terrah?"

"I-I'm not offended. Just taken aback."

Still in his arms, she could feel every hard muscle pressed against her body and it was making it difficult to construct a sentence in her head. Terrah realised he could make a liar out of her. She wanted to sleep with him, would go willingly to his bed if he so much as suggested it to her right now.

"Did my kiss convince you that my attraction for you is real? Maybe another — "

"No! I believe you."

Nick released her, but not before she'd felt the hard ridge of his cock against her.

"Good. Because we *will* see each other again."

Terrah didn't say anything as he bent down and grabbed her case. She could barely focus on what he was saying about the history of the aquarium as she followed him out of the room. Terrah willed her wobbly legs not to fail her as they walked back through the brightly lit lobby to the glass doors leading outside.

Nick held the door open for her before striding up to the first cab lined up outside the hotel.

"Well." Terrah placed one hand on the door as he opened it, lifting her chin to meet Nick's eyes. "It's been interesting, Nick Tasso."

"Likewise, Terrah Bryant."

They smiled at each other.

"Until next time."

Nick leaned into her, gifting her with another generous whiff of his cologne as he kissed her on the temple.

"Until next time."

Terrah slid into the car seat and waved through the glass as Nick closed the door and the cabbie pulled out into the traffic. She stared, unseeing, out of the window in a state of euphoria.

What a night.

Her grin faded.

They hadn't even exchanged phone numbers.

Damn.

Her fingers went up to touch her lips. They still seemed to tingle from Nick's kiss. A ribbon of desire wrapped around her body as she imagined him kissing her again. He had an absolute gift for the art of seductive lip-locking.

He didn't even ask me for my number.

Terrah sighed as she stared out of the window at the congested traffic. It was probably for the best. There was no telling what would happen between them if they were ever alone together again. The chemistry between them, from Terrah's perspective, was strip-naked-and-hit-the-sheets explosive and Nick had had no qualms about telling her it was the same for him. She was almost afraid to know what it would be like to explore that kind of sexual verve with someone.

Terrah shook her head, still in shock. Her friends would never believe she'd kissed international hottie model Nick Tasso. The cabbie swerved into another lane and she grabbed hold of the door handle as they zipped by another taxi. Terrah gazed out of the window and the magic of the evening seemed to fade with every passing city block.

Restless and flustered, Terrah sighed. Despite her self-drawn conclusion that having anything to do with Nick would be foolish, she couldn't help wondering if she'd run into him again.

There was a chance. The modelling world really wasn't that big.

Stop.

She'd had a nice dinner. It was best to leave it at that.

In a few days, she'd be in Hawaii for the first time. She would focus on the upcoming shoot and not the irrational...*ridiculous* longing to see Nick Tasso again.

Chapter Six

"Last call for Aloha Airlines, flight one-nineteen."

Terrah sighed as she got up from the hard chair she'd been sitting in for over an hour. She bit back a curse as her purse fell to the floor. Her nine-lives phone clinked on the grey linoleum.

Great…just great.

Stooping, Terrah swiped up her bag and stuffed her phone inside, not even bothering to see if it was functioning properly. She shoved the thick straps of her purse onto her shoulder, frustrated that she was now the very last person in line to board the plane.

Wait—there was a haggard-looking guy getting in line behind her who looked like she felt. Flying wasn't her favourite way to travel and she always liked getting to the airport on time, but nothing had gone right. Her taxi had been late picking her up, then the afternoon thunderstorm had seemed to make every commuter in New York even more insane. She'd arrived at the airport with not a moment to spare, then raced towards her terminal, hoping for a miracle—and her wish had been granted. Her plane had been delayed because of the storm.

Just keep telling yourself, in a few hours you'll be in sunny Hawaii.

Yes, but she had to *get* there first, and the delay because of the storm had only made her more nervous about flying.

Does anyone else fear for the safety of the plane?

Terrah glanced at the people in front of her, seeing and hearing nothing but smiling faces and excited conversation.

Apparently she was the only one inwardly freaking out.

The only good news was, maybe she could sleep through most of the ten-hour flight.

"Sorry about the delay. May I have your ticket, please?"

Terrah's gaze flicked over the ticket counter agent's name tag. She didn't think Joan looked very sorry about Terrah's numb behind, but she handed over her ticket.

"I'm sorry, Ms Bryant, it looks like this flight has been overbooked."

Terrah held her tongue as the guy behind her cursed, vehemently enough for the both of them.

Joan flashed him an impatient look before offering Terrah another apologetic smile.

"I can offer you a free ticket voucher, or perhaps you'd like to wait on standby for the next flight? The next one to Oahu leaves at six thirty-five in the morning."

Vouchers? Wait on standby?

She had to be on the Big Island in twenty hours!

"Can you upgrade us?" the bedraggled gentleman asked, moving up beside her at the counter.

Terrah glanced away from him to see Joan's eyes narrow.

"Please — I have to be on this flight." Terrah used her gentlest, friendliest, please-help-me-now voice.

"Let me take a look here" — the ticket agent's face seemed to soften as she started to tap on her keyboard — "and see what I can do."

Terrah exchanged a look with the guy who shared her predicament, and both of them waited with bated breath as Joan lifted her head from the computer screen.

"All right, Ms Bryant, you've been upgraded to business class. Go now to board the plane."

"What about me?" The harried man's voice had gone up a notch.

Relieved, Terrah took the ticket handed to her, tuning out Joan's tart response to the guy next to her as she walked forward. Arriving late in Hawaii would have not been good. She wanted time to unpack, get settled and relax before the photo shoot taking place tomorrow afternoon.

Now to just get through ten hours on the plane.

Terrah took a steady breath as she moved steadily forward, through the loud tunnel that led to the stewardess waiting to greet her.

"Welcome to Aloha Airlines, Ms Bryant. Let me take you to your seat."

She tried to ignore the butterflies skittering in her stomach as she walked onto the plane. Terrah followed the stewardess through the red curtains blocking out the rest of the passengers.

So this is how to travel in style.

No screaming children. No cramped three-in-a-row seating. There were two comfy seats to each row with plenty of leg room. Everyone looked comfortable and content. The stewardesses were actually smiling.

I've officially re-entered the Twilight Zone. It's called first class, baby.

"Terrah?"

That voice.

No way… Can't be!

Terrah's head whipped to the left and her eyes widened as her gaze fell upon Nick Tasso.

Her brain froze for a moment as he smiled at her, looking even more devilishly handsome than she wanted to remember.

"*Nick*, you're on this flight?"

It was a silly question.

He was obviously going to Hawaii on Aloha Airlines flight one-nineteen.

Terrah's heart hammered in her chest as Nick grinned at her.

"Yes, we're working on the same photo shoot. Why don't you join me? No one's sitting here," Nick said, motioning to the window seat beside him.

"Would you like me to stow your carry-on, Ms Bryant?"

"Yes, thank you."

Terrah handed the lady her shoulder bag before moving past Nick to get into her window seat. Her gaze ran over Nick as he sat back down.

Omigoodness, he's even hotter than I remembered.

He looked completely relaxed and undeniably sexy in worn jeans and a white button-down shirt that was open at the neck. The familiar scent of his cologne teased her, reminding her of their kiss the last time they'd been together as she settled into her leather seat.

"I missed my earlier flight and now I'm glad I did."

"I was upgraded at the last minute." Terrah smoothed her hair, wishing she'd had time to check her appearance in the bathroom before boarding the plane. "This is another unexpected surprise. I didn't know you were doing this shoot."

"It's a surprise to me, too" — Nick leaned in towards her — "but I told you we'd see each other again. I take this as a sign."

"A sign?"

She was captivated by the deep, low tones of his voice as he took her hand, brought it to his lips and kissed her wrist.

"Yes, a sign that you and I are destined to explore the chemistry between us. I've been thinking about you since our impromptu dinner date."

Terrah was speechless as he brushed his lips over her skin again, happy to know he'd been thinking about her — because she hadn't stopped thinking about him since the other night. She'd never confess it to Nick, but she'd replayed their conversation and his erotic kiss over and over in her mind.

"Did you think about me, Terrah?"

She pulled her hand from his. "I wondered if we'd see each other again."

It was all she could admit to at the moment. She made a big deal out of smoothing down her skirt, conscious of Nick's eyes on her. His unexpected presence and his direct question had thrown her for a loop.

"I wanted to call you before this trip, but I didn't get a chance."

"*And* you didn't have my number."

Terrah pressed her back into the seat in an effort to look more relaxed. Nick's hard thigh brushed against her leg and his aqua-green gaze fixed on her.

"Yes, I do, and I would've called if I hadn't known I'd see you in Hawaii."

She didn't bother to ask how he'd got her telephone number. It didn't matter. The only thing that did was the fact that he was now inches away from her. The erotic vibe between them, which she'd begun to doubt had even existed, was zapping her from head to toe all over again. It would be so easy to give in to it and let him seduce her.

Hell, she was ready to seduce *him*.

You don't date models, Terrah.

A self-imposed rule, but she'd been in the biz long enough to appreciate the old adage, 'You don't mix business with pleasure.' In truth, she'd never been tempted by any of the handsome men she'd worked with before, but Nick... Nick was tempting as hell.

"You look amazing."

"Thank you."

A flash of heat coursed through her as his gaze drifted over her lime-green, short-sleeved sweater top and her white pencil skirt. She'd chosen to wear the light sweater knowing it might be chilly on the plane. The scooped neckline showcased her favourite silver necklace and dangling lipstick pendant.

"Suddenly"—Nick leaned closer to her—"the ten-hour flight doesn't seem long enough."

Ten hours of sexual tension was going to drive her crazier than her fear of flying.

"Mmm...what perfume are you wearing?"

"Jasmine- and vanilla-scented body oil."

"I love it. You were wearing it the other night, weren't you?"

"Yes. It's my favourite."

"It's very sexy."

He had to know what he was doing to her.

"Thank you."

Her voice sounded breathy in her own ears, evidence of how fast her heart was pounding in her chest.

The light sweater had been the wrong choice.

She was *way* too hot.

There wasn't a chill in the world that could dampen the effect of Nick's smouldering charm coupled with the heat of his gaze.

"Excuse me."

They both directed their attention to the stewardess, breaking the erotically charged moment between them.

"Would either of you care for a warm towel?"

"Thank you," Terrah said, accepting the towel to wipe her hands.

She would've preferred a *cold* towel to cool off her heated face.

"Can we get two glasses of champagne?"

"Of course, Mr Tasso."

The stewardess smiled at him as she took their towels and went off to fulfil his request.

"Champagne?"

"We're celebrating."

"Celebrating what?"

"Us." Nick paused to thank the stewardess. "The two of us...here, right now." He took the two glasses offered and passed one to Terrah before lifting his glass. "Let's share a toast."

"A toast..." Terrah lifted her own glass, mesmerised by the mischievous gleam in Nick's eyes.

"To the unexpected."

* * * *

Nick watched Terrah as she clinked her glass against his. He sipped his champagne, thinking it didn't taste half as good as her lips.

God…he wanted to kiss her.

He almost *had* kissed her when she'd looked at him with those beautiful, big brown eyes filled with surprise.

It had taken quite a bit of self-control to watch her get in the cab the other night, when he'd wanted to ask her to stay. He'd been certain she wouldn't have turned him down, but he hadn't wanted her to have any regrets or to question his motives later. He'd known he'd see her again one way or another. As far as he was concerned, fate had intervened when he'd discovered they were both going to be doing the shoot in Hawaii.

Nick glanced over at Terrah, wondering how he was going to survive a ten-hour exercise in self-control. Her perfume alone was turning him on, and when he looked at her…

Holy hell.

She looked every bit as sexy as he remembered, and then some, in her white skirt that had outlined the delicious curve of her ass before she'd sat down. Her green sweater complemented her complexion while showing off her small waist and the more than generous swell of her breasts.

Nick shifted in his seat, remembering the kiss they'd shared by the aquarium, which made the blood race straight down to his cock.

Damn… Don't think about it. Don't even think about it.

The mental nudge wasn't enough to stop him from recalling how good Terrah had felt in his arms, but at least his semi hard-on was temporarily on standby.

"Like the champagne?"

Terrah nodded as she finished a sip. "It's delicious. I'm hoping it'll take the edge off before we take off."

"Don't like flying?"

His gaze drifted down to her manicured fingertips as she tapped them on her skirt.

"Let's just say I prefer to keep both feet on the ground."

"Don't worry. I've flown to Hawaii several times. It's a long flight, but we will arrive safely."

Terrah pinned him with a serious look he found utterly adorable.

"You *can't* be certain of that. Anything can happen."

"True. But we can't live our lives in fear of what *might* happen."

He took another sip from his glass as Terrah frowned at him.

She crossed her legs, drawing his attention away from her face to her shapely calf muscles and her wedge sandals. Her toenails sported the same pale lilac hue as her fingernails.

"I don't live my life in fear. I just don't like flying, especially when it's stormy."

"Well, I'm glad I'm on this flight with you, then. I'll keep you distracted until we reach those beautiful, sandy shores."

The sassy smile Terrah gave him brought to mind all kinds of naughty ways he could keep her distracted until they landed.

Keep up this train of thought and you're in trouble.

Nick glanced at his watch.

Ten hours.

Ten hours of sitting next to Terrah and not touching her? Pure torture.

One thing was for sure—he hadn't been this attracted to a woman in a long, long time.

"Hawaii is gorgeous. I hope we both get some time to enjoy the island."

Together.

He didn't say it, but he was going to make sure it happened. They were going to explore the sizzling chemistry between them.

"Can I take your glasses?"

Nick took Terrah's empty glass and handed it to the stewardess, along with his own.

"I've always wanted to go to Hawaii." Terrah sighed. "Once we get off this plane, I can't wait to see if it's as gorgeous as everyone always says."

"You'll love it."

They both looked up as another flight attendant started on the safety speech.

Nick admired the dark wild curls brushing against Terrah's shoulders as she listened intently to the stewardess.

"You're not paying attention," she whispered, without looking at him.

"I already know the location of my flotation device."

He winked at her, amused by her fierce glare before she returned her focus to the stewardess, who was finishing up. Shortly thereafter, the captain announced they were about to take off.

"So, how's your phone?"

"My phone has been replaced."

"So it *was* damaged by the fall."

"No, I just decided to finally get a new one. I think I was the last person in New York with an older model."

He watched Terrah dig inside her purse and pull out the new, sleek, rectangular device.

"Now, I just have to figure out how to use all the stuff on it."

Nick was aware of the pressure in the cabin changing as the engines started kicking into high gear. He leaned over Terrah to look out of the window. "The lights over the city are going to look amazing as we take off."

"I'll take your word for it."

The building hum within the plane increased when it taxied down the runaway, and they both settled back in their seats.

Nick observed Terrah gripping the side of her chair with one hand. The whirr of the engines reached a fevered pitch and the stiffness of her posture spoke volumes as the plane jettisoned forward. She tensed beside him, and he knew exactly what to do to take her mind off their takeoff.

"Terrah?"

The moment she turned her face towards him, he claimed her lips in a gentle kiss. He cradled her chin with his hand, half expecting her to pull away, but she melted instead, parting her lips to let him in. The tension within her body lessened as he stroked the side of her face with his thumb. He loved the feel of her soft skin beneath his fingertips as her tongue caressed and teased, mimicking his movements. She tasted of champagne. His cock, which had been behaving, instantly hardened as he imagined tasting all of her.

When he finally broke the kiss, they were in the air.

Chapter Seven

Terrah slowly opened her eyes to stare at him.

His gaze fell from her luscious lips to her heaving breasts, his dick stiffening almost to the point of pain in his jeans when he saw the outline of her hard nipples protruding through her thin sweater.

She wanted him as much as he wanted her. He'd known that already, but confirmation was always good.

Very good.

He wanted to give her whatever she wanted.

"Refills?"

The interruption gave him a chance to shift in the chair, casually adjusting his shirt over his erection.

"Definitely."

Nick took the glass as Terrah cleared her throat.

"I think I'll have another glass, too."

After Terrah took her drink, they both thanked the stewardess and she moved on.

Nick took a generous swallow, aware of Terrah's eyes on him.

"You kissed me to distract me as the plane was taking off?"

"Yes. Did it help?"

Terrah seemed embarrassed as she took a sip from her glass. Nick could tell she was searching for the right thing to say when she looked at him.

"Yes, it did."

"Good. I'm glad my kiss could help."

Help?

She was in serious trouble.

In danger of spontaneously combusting in mid-air!

His kiss alone makes me wet.

Her panties were drenched and her pulse was racing as her body tried to come down off the sexual high that was Nick Tasso.

God, the things he could do with his mouth.

She couldn't imagine those lips anywhere else on her body.

Liar!

Okay, so she could imagine it. *Was* imagining it right now, as he calmly sipped his champagne as if he hadn't just shown her, again, how an honest-to-goodness passion-filled kiss was done.

"Look, you can see the skyline." Nick gestured towards the plane window.

Terrah turned her head to see the twinkling lights of the city below for a second, before clouds obscured their view. She pressed back into her seat with a shaky breath.

"Do you need another kiss?"

Yes!

"Ha ha! Very funny."

"I'm very serious."

Terrah smiled. "I'll let you know."

"Don't be shy. I'm always ready to help."

He grinned at her and she couldn't help but laugh.

Nick was right... Ten hours suddenly didn't seem that long.

She looked past him to their stewardess, who gave them both a warm smile.

"Dinner will be served shortly. Would you two prefer the roasted chicken with saffron rice or our red snapper with Caesar salad?"

"Chicken."

"Salad," Terrah said a nanosecond after Nick's response.

The flight attendant chuckled. "Okay, will you be having more champagne with dinner?"

Terrah shook her head. "Just water for me."

Nick smiled at the stewardess. "Same here."

He turned to her when they were alone. "Are you hungry?"

"A little. How 'bout you?"

She saw something flicker in his eyes—longing? Desire? She couldn't be sure, but her body reacted instantly, heating up all over again.

"I could eat."

You.

His gaze never left her face and his eyes spoke to her as clearly as if he'd whispered in her ear. For a brief moment, Terrah wondered if he'd actually spoken the word that popped into her head, except his lips hadn't moved. He was a master at conveying his thoughts with his body language and those sexy eyes. Her heart skipped a beat as she pictured him licking her nipples, which were brushing against the soft cotton of her bra, erect, ready for his tongue. She shivered, imagining him leaving a trail of kisses down the valley between her breasts to her pussy.

Water.

She needed water right now to put out the fire he was building within her with no real effort at all.

"Are you cold?" He knew damn well she wasn't.

She was saved from answering as their food arrived.

They were served their dinners and her breathing slowly returned to normal. Nick kept her talking while they ate their meal, which turned out to be delicious. Who knew airline food could actually be tasty?

Terrah found herself laughing easily with Nick. They chatted about work stuff and mutual acquaintances, which helped her to stop obsessing over every dip of the plane. An unexpected thrill of delight zipped through her every time he chuckled at something she said.

She loved the sound of his deep voice, but his laugh was positively delicious!

It really wasn't fair for him to be so damned sexy *and* easy-going. He was one of the top male models in the world, yet he was the most unpretentious man in the industry she knew.

Their plates were taken away and they both settled back in their seats.

"Well" — Nick glanced at his watch — "only seven hours and thirty-four minutes until we land."

"Don't remind me."

Her gaze dropped to his mouth as he smiled.

She suddenly longed to taste his kiss again. Heat suffused her face as she averted her attention to her purse.

Distraction… You need a distraction.

She pulled out a fashion magazine she'd bought at the airport, flipped it open and casually turned the pages. Her eyes widened as she stopped and stared at the glossy page.

So much for distraction.

There was Nick in all his male beauty, lounging on a beautiful leather couch in only his designer underwear.

Terrah groaned softly as her eyes feasted on the lust-inducing ad.

The camera angle and expert lighting lovingly highlighted every sinewy line and hard muscle. Nick's body was a work of art in itself. The noticeable bulge in the underwear held her attention for a moment, but it was the smouldering look in his eyes that tempted her. His electrifying gaze held a million promises and Terrah was willing to bet he could fulfil every one of them.

She turned the page, casting a quick glance at Nick who was busy fiddling with his phone. It didn't look like he'd just seen her ogling his picture.

Thank goodness.

Taking a deep breath, Terrah began reading an article on how to expertly trim eyebrows. She was halfway through it when Nick cleared his throat.

"So…"

She lifted her head from the magazine to look at him. "So?"

"Tell me what you were you thinking about when you saw my ad."

Damn! He *had* seen her.

"Nice underwear."

Nick raised an eyebrow.

"That's *all* you were thinking about?"

His voice was lower than normal as he leaned a little closer to her. She had to lift her chin higher to meet his eyes.

"C'mon, Nick"—Terrah shook her head with an exasperated sigh—"I was thinking about what I'm sure *every* woman on this planet thinks about when looking at that picture."

Was he for real?

Did he really think she was going to confess all her secret erotic fantasies about him to his face?

"I'm not interested in knowing what every other woman is thinking, only you."

His seductive tone captivated her as she held his gaze.

"I'm sure you can guess what I was thinking about, Nick."

"I'm not a mind reader. Were you admiring the boxers? Were you studying lighting or maybe the backdrop? Or...were you imagining the two of us together in bed?"

A wave of desire crested over her, so strong that Terrah squeezed her thighs together as if the small movement could prevent the flood of wetness from soaking her panties.

"What kind of question is that?" The moist heat centring between her legs competed with the burn of her cheeks.

"The kind of question I want an answer to."

"Yes. I was imagining what it would be like to have sex with you."

She had hoped to shock him with her brazen response, but he simply nodded his head as if she'd just commented on the weather. Terrah averted her face, feeling exposed and ridiculous as she picked an imaginary piece of lint off her skirt.

Why had she admitted that to him?

He's still staring at m—

"Let me tell you what it would be like."

Heaven help me.

She whipped her head up, her eyes widening as she met Nick's steady gaze.

"I'd tease you first and make you come."

She gasped as he shifted in his seat, turning his body slightly so that the passengers across from them were blocked.

He leaned toward her. "When you were ready, I'd take you slow." He lowered his voice even more. "I'd want to see every expression on your face as I fucked you."

"Nick, please!" Terrah yanked on the neck of her sweater, hotter and wetter than she'd ever been in her life.

"Yeah, and I'd want you to say my name. I promise I'd *make* you say my name over and over again. Like you just did…only on the edge of a scream—"

"Nick!"

He gave her a rueful smile, as if he'd got carried away and regretted speaking, but Terrah knew better.

"Do you have a clear picture of what it'd be like now?"

Terrah blinked, rendered speechless by the scorching hot mental picture Nick had painted with his bold words.

He was so sure it was going to happen.

And it is.

Liquid fire coursed through her veins instead of blood as she tried to swallow the lump in her throat. She fidgeted in her chair, wishing she could get some fresh air or least take a breath without smelling Nick's pheromone-laden cologne.

"Terrah…"

He said her name in lowered, husky tones, as if they were already in bed, making her squirm even more in her seat as she averted her face from his to look out of the window.

She was going to break her own rule about dating models.

And who said anything about dating?

This was probably only going to be a brief fling. A brief, hot, *wild* fling. She'd worry about her shattered principles once she got back home. Terrah still wasn't convinced Nick wasn't just a player used to getting whichever woman he wanted in bed. There was a huge chance she'd get played, but it was a risk she was willing to take because she wanted him more than she'd wanted any other man in her life.

Nick's gentle caress on her arm snapped her out of her thoughts. She looked at him, sucking in a breath as he chuckled.

"I'll take your silence as a yes."

She could only stare at him as he gave her an amused smile. Terrah closed her eyes for a brief moment as Nick turned his attention to their ever-attentive stewardess. She exhaled, wishing she'd come up with a pithy response, but it was hard to deny the truth. There had to be laws in place against men who had this much sex appeal and charm. The stewardess wasn't immune either, laughing and smiling with Nick as she offered him two blankets. She watched him take them, her eyes drawn to his fingers on the soft blue material.

Even his hands are beautiful.

And she wanted them all over her body.

The erotic thoughts filling her head made her stomach dip, and the plane seemed to emulate the motion as Nick handed over her blanket.

"Did you feel that?"

Nick nodded. "A little turbulence, nothing to fear."

"Righ—"

Terrah stopped short as the captain's voice came over the speaker.

"This is your captain speaking. Just wanted to let you know we may encounter a few pockets of bad weather. We should be through it shortly. Please keep your seatbelts fastened until further notice."

Pockets of bad weather…

Was that a nice way of saying 'Be prepared for an emergency landing'?

Terrah glanced up to where the oxygen masks were supposed to fall down. She needed to relax. There was nothing to fear.

"Terrah."

Nothing to fear at all. You're just a few thousand feet above the Pacific Ocean.

"Terrah, look at me."

She slowly turned toward Nick.

"You're not going to freak out on me over a little turbulence, are you?"

"What? No. I'm good."

"You're not good. I can practically see the disaster scenarios playing out in that pretty head of yours." Nick reached out and touched her knee. "Am I going to have to kiss you until that 'Fasten your seatbelt' sign goes off? Because I will."

Terrah laughed. "That might bother the people across from us."

"Do you think I'm concerned about that?"

He traced a circle on her knee, shifting all of her attention away from the integrity of the plane and back to him. Tension faded from her shoulders as the warmth of his touch spread like wildfire up her leg.

Nick tapped his finger on her thigh. "Why don't we watch a movie?"

"A movie sounds good."

It felt strange talking about watching a movie as if he hadn't just declared his intention to take her to bed for sweet loving.

"Comedy? Drama? Romance?"

The tone of his voice darkened a little on the last word and Terrah dropped her gaze from his face to his hand, which was still on her knee.

"Definitely not drama."

"Let's laugh, then."

He slipped his hand off her leg, and Terrah watched him set up the movie.

"What did you pick?"

"It's a surprise."

He grinned at her as he put on his headphones.

Terrah followed suit and looked at the screen in front of her. She groaned when Jim Carrey popped up on the screen. Within minutes she was giggling at the actor's wild antics, totally forgetting about her fears concerning the plane.

It felt perfectly natural laughing and watching the movie with Nick, who seemed to find the same things as funny as she did. She was actually enjoying herself...in the air.

Terrah glanced at Nick, taking in the way his long frame lounged back in his seat. He was the reason she was so relaxed, and she appreciated his efforts to help her calm down. Her gaze ran over his white shirt and she wished she could lay her head on his chest. She could—she knew it, he wouldn't stop her—but the seats weren't conducive to that kind of arrangement.

Too bad.

Or maybe it was for the best.

The more she contemplated sleeping with Nick, the more she realised she might not be able to walk away from him unscathed. She kept discovering new things she liked about him besides his good looks. Spending more time with him confirmed she was more than just physically attracted to him.

Halfway through the film, Terrah found it harder and harder to keep her eyes open. She pushed her seat back and turned her body towards Nick to stretch out into a more comfortable position. She inhaled deeply and a yawn escaped from her lips. Her eyelids fluttered downward as she fought to stay awake. She smiled sleepily, unable to stop Nick's erotic declarations from replaying in her head.

Terrah wondered if he was a man of his word. She wanted to find out in the worst way.

She was exhausted and sex-deprived…clearly in no shape to rationally think about all the ramifications of sleeping with Nick.

Her eyelids dropped and the last thing she saw was Nick's gorgeous profile illuminated by the screen in front of him as she drifted off to sleep.

Chapter Eight

"Terrah..."

Nick watched the blanket slip from Terrah's shoulders as she shifted in her seat. She looked so damned beautiful while sleeping. Her soft moan made his cock twitch and it took considerable effort not to touch her. He was certain she'd welcome his caresses, but he didn't want to start something that couldn't be finished thirty thousand feet in the air.

When he touched her again he wanted no interruptions...nothing stopping him from doing exactly what he'd told her he would, what he'd been thinking about for the past ten hours.

"Terrah, wake up."

She opened her eyes, blinking as she arched her body.

His gazed dropped briefly to her breasts, which were pushing invitingly against the soft threads of her sweater. If she'd been any other woman, he'd have thought she'd orchestrated the movement for his benefit, but Terrah wasn't like any other woman. She was simply loosening the kinks from her body.

And I want to work 'em out for her.

"What time is it?"

Nick glanced at his watch. "Almost six in New York, but we're about to land and it's almost eleven here."

As if on cue, the captain came on the air, announcing their estimated landing time in Hawaii.

"You slept through breakfast service. Are you hungry?"

Terrah shook her head, setting her seat back into the upright position. "I'm just ready to get off this plane. Did you sleep?"

"A little. I never sleep well on planes."

"Me either, typically."

Nick grinned. "Could've fooled me. You were snoring the whole time."

Terrah's eyes widened with horror. "Are you serious?"

"No."

She glared at him. "I don't do jokes before eight a.m."

"We're on Hawaiian time now, sweetheart."

Their stewardess stopped and offered coffee, which they both accepted.

Nick took a sip, appreciating the strong brew. In truth, he hadn't slept that much at all. Being so close to Terrah without being able to caress her had acted as a natural stimulant, keeping him awake for most of the flight.

A few minutes later, their coffee cups were picked up and the seatbelt warning sign came on, signalling their impending landing.

"Not long now. How are you during plane landings? Should I be ready to distract you?"

Terrah laughed. "I'm too excited to freak out right now. We're finally here! And we have the rest of this day to relax a little before tomorrow's shoot."

Pity. He wouldn't have minded kissing her until the plane came to a complete stop.

"I can't wait to take a nice, long shower."

Nick watched Terrah twist a curl around her finger before reaching for her purse.

Have mercy!

Terrah in the shower. Her innocent statement sparked his imagination in a hundred different naughty ways.

Terrah naked and wet…

Nick cleared his throat. "Will you let me take you to brunch?"

Her lips curved up as she applied lip gloss. The shimmering, rosy hue made her full lips look even more kissable.

Suckable.

"Mmm…brunch sounds great."

Nick loved Terrah's smile—so sexy and cute at the same time.

Soon, the plane touched down and in no time at all they were exiting the aircraft together. They were greeted by four lovely Hawaiian women who placed fragrant leis around their necks before they entered the airport terminal.

"I can't believe I'm in Hawaii!"

Her excitement made him grin.

"Let's get our luggage, so we can check into our hotel."

He led the way to baggage claim, ignoring the stares and random camera flashes directed at him.

"You've obviously got some major fans here."

Nick shrugged. "I'm sure news about the shoot has spread all over the island. Look, the luggage is coming out."

"There's mine."

"The brown suitcase with the red tie?"

"Yep."

"I'll get it."

He left her side, reaching the bag right before it would've disappeared on the conveyor belt. His own luggage appeared seconds later.

"Thanks," Terrah said, taking the handle from him. "Now to get a taxi."

"I'm sure there's a limo waiting for me."

Terrah lifted her head up in acknowledgment. "Right."

"Come on."

He led the way again, through the busy terminal towards the doors, where a man with his name on a sign stood waiting. The limo driver recognised him instantly, rushing over with a smile to take Terrah's suitcase.

"Aloha, Mr Tasso. My name's Tim. Welcome back to Hawaii."

"Thank you, Tim. Just call me Nick, and this is Terrah — she'll be accompanying me to the hotel."

"Of course. Let me take your bags."

Tim ushered them through the doors and Nick took in a deep breath of the warm, fresh air as they approached the sleek black limo. Within minutes they were pulling away from the kerb. He pointed out a few buildings to Terrah as they made their way to the hotel, enjoying being the tour guide. Terrah's enthusiasm was infectious. She listened intently to every bit of information he shared about the island.

The car finally came to a stop in front of their hotel. They got out of the vehicle and Nick smiled as Terrah gasped.

"The hotel is beautiful!"

"It's one of the finest," Tim said, taking their luggage out of the trunk. "Enjoy your stay here on the Big Island."

Terrah beamed. "Thank you."

"*Mahalo*," Nick said, tipping the driver as the bellboy took their luggage. He turned to Terrah. "Ready to check in?"

"Yes!"

Nick held open the door to the hotel lobby and Terrah walked through.

"I love the flowers! Look at those gorgeous blossoms." She gestured towards the large display of exotic blossoms filling the lobby.

"They'll have fresh flowers in your room, too."

"You've stayed here before?"

Nick nodded. "I was here last year."

"You were on location for a shoot?" Terrah asked as they approached the front desk.

"Yes."

"*Aloha*, welcome to Alkii Hotel, Mr Tasso. Your room is ready. I'll just need to see your ID and a major credit card."

Nick handed over the required items, then pocketed his room key as Terrah stepped up to the other clerk, who was ready to check her in.

"Terrah, Nick, you made it."

Nick turned around to see Aidan striding towards them, with his full attention on Terrah.

"Hello, Aidan."

Aidan?

Since when was Terrah on a first-name basis with Aidan Marks?

"Good to see you, Nick."

"How long have you been here?" Nick asked, shaking the other man's hand.

Aidan grinned. "Since Saturday. FYI, the shoot has been pushed forward one hour for tomorrow. I want to take full advantage of all the natural light. The spot I've picked out is amazing."

"I can't wait to see it."

Aidan glanced at his phone, then back at Terrah.

"Terrah, I'm sure you want to get settled, but can I snatch you away for just a moment?"

Nick met Terrah's gaze. "We'll meet up in about an hour?"

Aidan smiled at Nick as Terrah nodded. "I'll see *you* tomorrow. Don't stay up too late. I need you at the top of your game tomorrow, pretty boy."

"You got it," Nick said, forcing a grin he didn't feel.

Jerk.

He walked away from Aidan and Terrah and headed towards the lift.

Aidan Marks was a fantastic photographer, but he could be an ass and one thing was certain—he had a thing for Terrah. Nick had picked up on the other man's attraction to Terrah and he didn't like it. And he was certain there was a familiarity between the two of them, too.

Just how well did she know Aidan?

* * * *

Terrah tore her gaze from Nick as the doors to the elevator he'd stepped into closed, and gave her full attention to Aidan.

"I know Michelle told you the theme for the shoot, but the client decided to go with the god and goddesses concept at the last minute. I knew you'd come equipped for anything, but I wanted to give you a heads-up."

"Thanks. The concept change won't be a problem. I look forward to the creative challenge," Terrah said, mentally cataloguing the makeup she would need for the shoot. She was confident there would be no need to hit a cosmetic store.

"How was your flight in?"

"Long, but otherwise uneventful."

Not true...so not true! Flashbacks of Nick kissing her on the plane ran through her mind.

"I saw you walk in with Nick—"

"We were on the same flight."

Aidan lifted one eyebrow. "Oh? Did I just hear dinner plans?"

"Possibly." Terrah was slightly annoyed the conversation had turned from business matters and on to her personal life.

"Well, if you find yourself free...have dinner with me."

"Thanks for the invitation, Aidan. I'll probably just go up to my room and relax. I want to be fresh and inspired for you tomorrow morning."

Aidan nodded. "All right, but I do hope we can share a meal together while we're here on the island."

"Sounds good. I'll see you tomorrow morning."

"Don't be late."

"Not a chance."

She smiled at him before turning on her heel. There was a bellboy already waiting with her luggage as she walked back past the front desk. She followed him to the lift, anxious to shed her travel clothes and freshen up.

The bellboy held the elevator doors open for her and she stepped inside, suppressing a sigh of frustration.

She had no intentions of making dinner plans with Aidan. All she could think about was Nick.

Nick.

Where was he?

Her phone vibrated in her purse and she dug for it while the doors to the elevator opened. She followed the bellboy down the hallway and glanced at her cell.

She had a text message from Nick.

Room 910 in one hour.

Her heart raced with excitement. She tipped and thanked the bellhop with a barely contained grin.

They were on the same floor. She was in room nine-oh-five.

Pressing her electronic key into the slot, she breathed a sigh of relief as the door to her room swung open. She slipped out of her heels, padded to the window and inhaled the heady scent of flowers. Her room was lovely, the décor evoking a sense of escapism with a taste of the exotic. She had a gorgeous view of the pool and she stood for a moment, staring down at the people lounging and swimming, obviously enjoying the weather and water.

After stripping out of her clothes, she unzipped her suitcase and extracted her favourite body wash. She pinned up her hair and headed to the bathroom, appreciating the spaciousness and simplistic design of the facility as she turned on the shower. Once the water was at the perfect temperature, she stepped beneath the massaging stream.

She was more excited about spending time with Nick than she was about the photo shoot that would no doubt advance her career. The fragrant scent of her soap enveloped her as she lathered her skin and rinsed the bubbles away. She turned the water off, stepped out of the shower and mentally selected what to wear while wrapping herself in a big, fluffy towel.

Something sexy…but not too sexy.

She blow-dried her hair until the wild, ebony curls were straight enough to pull back into a somewhat tamed ponytail. Satisfied with her 'do, she padded back towards the bed, where her suitcase lay open, and pulled out a deceptively simple, white sundress. The A-line design complemented her generous curves. She loved the plunging cut in the dress that exposed her back, and the straps ensured she wouldn't be too hot if they dined outside.

Terrah reached for her perfume oil and smiled as she recalled Nick's compliment about her favourite scent. She dabbed it on all her pulse points before slipping on her black strapless bra and matching panties. She slid the dress on and shimmied it over her hips before stepping into her new, red, peep-toe heels. Terrah moved to the full-length mirror on the front of the bathroom door. Pivoting, she looked at her reflection from all angles before breaking out into a satisfied smile. The dress was designed to highlight a woman's body and it was doing its job damn well. Her breasts filled out the top and the material hugged her rounded bottom. The contrasting colour popped against her brown skin.

Not bad.

"Too much?" she mused out loud, twirling around one more time.

No way. She wanted Nick to find her irresistible — as irresistible as she found him.

Chapter Nine

Terrah stepped outside her room and headed down the hall towards Nick's. Her red heels made no sound on the soft carpet as she walked. She squeezed her red clutch purse and tried to ignore the butterflies fluttering in her chest. She stopped in front of the door marked 910, took a deep breath, and smoothed her hands down the sides of her dress one more time before knocking.

The door swung open much too soon.

Nick stood before her, freshly shaven and breathtakingly handsome, dressed in white linen pants and a black shirt that clung to his muscled arms.

"Wow! You look incredible."

"Thank you." Terrah smiled, suddenly breathless and wired. "So do you. Are you ready to go eat?"

The smile he gave her melted her bones, making it very difficult to stand with poise.

"Are you?"

They stared at one another for a second.

Terrah swallowed hard and nodded. "I'm starved."

Her voice was a whisper and she could barely hear herself speak over the wild roar of her thudding heart.

"So am I."

"What do you have a taste for?"

The answer flashed in his eyes. Nick reached for her, yanked her hard against his body and kissed her. She parted her mouth as he dragged her into his room. The door shut silently behind them and her purse fell to the floor. His arm tightened around her waist, their lips melded and Terrah moaned with need. The force of attraction between them could no longer be denied. She wanted him to take her...make her scream his name as he had promised her she would. Nick shifted his lips from hers and the sound of their hurried breathing filled the room.

"Nick..."

"Don't tell me to stop." His voice was ragged and dark as he backed her up towards the bed.

"I wouldn't dare."

"I want you so bad, Terrah."

His words and his hands on her body made her want to show him she felt the same way. She tugged at his shirt, lifting it up over his head as he raised his arms.

"I want you, too."

Nick slipped the straps of her dress off her shoulders, and Terrah shivered as it fell to the floor in a soft heap around her feet.

"Look at you." His heated gaze swept over her from head to toe. "You're so damned beautiful. I love your body."

"Tell me what you love, Nick." Terrah reached out to touch his chest as he traced a line across the top of her breasts.

"These curves. The way you feel in my arms."

Terrah moaned as he gripped her hips and kissed her.

"I want to taste every inch of you. Touch me... Feel how much I want you."

She trembled as he took her hand and pressed it against the thin fabric of his pants. The feel of his thick erection beneath her fingers made her wet as she untied the drawstring.

Nick stepped out of them, pushed his underwear down over his narrow hips and her gaze dipped from his chiselled profile to his cock. He was so hard. She couldn't resist touching him again, sans clothing.

"Wait."

Terrah shook her head. "I can't." She protested as he moved away from her to go to his suitcase, which was lying on the coffee table by the bed. Her eyes drank in the naked sight of him as he extracted a condom. He ripped it open and returned to her side.

This was what she wanted. *He* was what she wanted.

"Allow me."

She took the condom from him, emboldened by his predatory grin. He slipped his fingers around her back to unfasten her bra. The scrap of material fluttered to the floor and Terrah bit her lip when Nick took a small step back to look at her. Every nerve in her body tingled beneath his silent appraisal. With his gaze on her breasts, she felt feverish and spellbound by the darkening hue of his eyes.

"I've wanted to touch you like this since the moment I laid eyes on you."

A gasp escaped her lips as he cupped the heavy mounds and toyed with her pebbled nipples. She returned the favour by rubbing her palm over the head of his glistening cock.

"I didn't believe you at first." Terrah lifted her damp hand to her face and tasted the wet spot as Nick watched.

"But you believe me now?"

"Yes."

In the blink of an eye, he had her wet hand pinned behind her back. He pulled her hair out of its ponytail with his free hand, and Terrah placed her other palm on his hard chest as he kissed her again. She could barely breathe as he crushed her to him, promising her erotic delights with his tongue in a demanding kiss that had them both breathless when he pulled away.

"No more teasing, Nick." She centred the condom over the head of his dick and gently sheathed him.

"Remember what I told you on the plane?" Nick asked, pushing her back on the bed.

She lay down on top of the comforter and he joined her, moving up between her legs with his cock pressed torturously against her panty-clad pussy.

"I remember."

He bent his head, and Terrah drew in a sharp breath as his tongue laved one of her taut nipples.

"What did I say?"

She stared up at him, unconsciously moving her pelvis against his hard length as he gently suckled on one erect peak.

"You told me you'd tease me first and make me come."

"I" — he sampled the other nipple with his hot mouth — "am a man of my word."

Terrah moaned, weaving her fingers through his thick, dark hair as he slid up to kiss the side of her neck.

"Are you ready for me, Terrah?"

His warm breath caressed her earlobe.

"*So* ready for you..."

She closed her eyes, enjoying each tactile sensation when Nick abruptly shifted his weight so he was kneeling between her legs. He yanked her bottom closer to his knees and she gasped again. Green eyes held hers and Terrah inhaled sharply when he palmed her wet heat through the sheer fabric of her panties. Terrah's breath hitched in her throat when he used one of his fingers to push the soft fabric into her slick folds.

"Nick, please..."

He stroked her swollen clit through her panties and she gripped the thick comforter beneath them.

"Please, what?"

"Please make me come."

Nick lifted the wet panties up from her trimmed pussy and ripped through the crotch, exposing her fully. He kept his eyes on her and a shudder coursed through her when his finger delved into her wetness again. Nick caressed her and a soft whimper escaped from her lips. She wanted more. Terrah spread her thighs wider, wanting to make sure he could properly taste her. She cried out when his warm mouth made contact with her drenched flesh. Her fragile control shattered as his tongue flicked over her super-sensitive clit. She loosened her grip on the comforter to press his head into her wetness, undulating her hips with pleasure from his onslaught of kisses on her pussy. Her gasps of pleasure grew louder as he began suckling her clit and penetrating her with his finger.

"Nick!"

Terrah clutched strands of his hair as he added another finger, preparing her for him. He simulated the movement of his cock with long, deep strokes. Faster and faster, his fingers worked in and out of her and Terrah began to whimper. Every cell in her body rushed toward a sweet, cataclysmic end. The array of erotic sensations overwhelmed her and she screamed as she came, trembling with each orgasmic ripple that tore through her. Nick continued lapping at her clit with unerring gentleness and persistence, wrenching every last ounce of pleasure to be had from her.

Writhing with pleasure, Terrah moaned incoherently as Nick's fingers slipped from her body. She felt him shift his weight again, moving over her, positioning his cock to take her at last. Her eyelids fluttered open again when he entered her. He slowly filled her and a long blissful sigh escaped her lips. She lifted her legs up to take him in even deeper. He kissed the side of her knee and she was touched by the tender gesture.

"You feel so good inside of me."

Her gaze locked with his, and she could see the depth of his passion for her in his eyes.

"It gets better than this," Nick ground out, proving his statement to be true with every thrust of his hips.

Terrah gripped his forearms, her fingers bit into his skin and she cried out again. Her voice echoed in the room along with the erotic sound of his body slamming against her with each measured stroke. He rocked her harder and she raked her fingers across his back, mewling with each skin-slapping thrust. Terrah crossed over into a world of pure ecstasy and realised pleasure had been only the beginning. Nick sank into her silky heat over and over again and she forgot all other coherent thoughts. She couldn't be quiet, didn't recognise the breathy sounds of bliss she was making. He momentarily silenced her whimpers with a kiss that pushed her back towards the ultimate pinnacle of release.

She hadn't thought another orgasm was possible during lovemaking. Her body proved her wrong. Nick pumped even faster and she climaxed again. Delicious ripples of pleasure stole her breath away. Terrah opened her mouth to scream again but she couldn't utter a sound.

"Terrah…"

Hearing his rough, passion-filled voice as he came did something to her heart, but there was no time to analyse it. She could only feel. Her body was Nick's and he'd taken her to a place she'd never been before. An erotic playground she'd never dreamed existed.

He slipped from her wet warmth to lie beside her. Sated and sweaty, all Terrah could do was pant, still coming down from her erotic high. For several minutes, there was nothing but the uneven sound of their heavy breathing in the bedroom.

"Wow!" Nick chuckled as he stretched against her. "I thought I'd imagined how incredible being with you would be but that was better than any fantasy."

Terrah smiled, basking in the languid glow of two incredible climaxes. Nick shifted on his side to face her and she turned her face towards him. He lifted his head up and rested his jaw in his hand.

"I agree."

I'll compare every lover to you…from this moment, forever.

"Mmm…" Terrah stretched her body out against his. "This was way better than brunch."

"It was, but I think we need to get some food."

"I don't want to move."

Terrah stretched slowly, loving the feel of his warm skin against hers.

"You don't have to. I'll order in. What do you have a taste for?" He winked at her as he swung out of the bed, and Terrah laughed.

"I'll never hear that question again and not think of this moment."

Nick flashed her a grin, walked to the coffee table and picked up the menu. Terrah admired the rippling muscles in his back. Her gaze drifted down over his tapered hips to his tight ass.

God, just watching him order room service was a sensory delight.

"I think I know what you want." Nick lifted the phone to his ear and glanced at her.

Terrah smiled as he started talking on the phone. Spying her ponytail holder lying on the carpet, she scooted off the comforter and picked it up. She pulled her hair up into a ponytail and headed for the bathroom. Her body felt deliciously tender all over. A hot shower was exactly what she needed to smooth out the tender aches.

You've got his sweat all over you.

The thought made her smile wider. She hadn't expected to sleep with him the moment he'd opened the door. The building sexual tension between them had exploded before she'd been able to overthink her wanton actions.

Naughty girl.

But at least now she could think about something other than Nick jumping her bones, like how beautiful and spacious his suite. He even had a deck furnished with lounge chairs and lush potted plants. She flipped on the bathroom light, not surprised to see a Jacuzzi tub as well as a walk-in shower in the contemporarily styled facility.

Terrah stared at her reflection in the huge mirror. She still had on her ripped panties. Remembering how Nick had torn them to taste her turned her on again. She reached for a washcloth inside the linen closet, stripped out of the soaked lingerie and padded to the shower. Once the water was warm, she stepped under the soothing stream and squeezed a dollop of shower gel from the bottle sitting on the marble shelf beside her. The fresh scent saturated the steam as she quickly lathered and rinsed off.

The sound of music greeted her ears as she turned off the water, stepped out of the shower and wrapped a towel around her body. She tucked it under her arm and peered into the steam-covered mirror.

So much for my hair.

Her sleek, blow-dried tresses were giving in to the humidity, curling in defiance.

"Done already?" Nick asked, entering the bathroom. "I was hoping to join you."

"Next time."

Terrah looked at him through the fogged mirror. She turned around, and her pulse quickened at the sight of his naked body.

"I'm going to hold you to that." Nick winked at her before turning the shower back on.

"I want you to."

Chapter Ten

Terrah watched Nick as he bent down, picked her panties up off the floor and lifted them up to his nose.

"You owe me a pair of panties." Her voice sounded husky, a result of latent desire surging full force again.

Nick smiled as he embraced her. "I suppose these are completely ruined." He pitched the ripped lace on the bathroom counter.

"Mm-hmm."

Terrah looked up at him, enjoying the feel of his strong arms wrapped around her. She rose up on her tiptoes and kissed his chin when he brushed his lips against her temple. "You shower so we can eat, because you're gonna need your strength."

"You think so?"

He stared down at her, and one dark eyebrow lifted as he squeezed her ass through the towel.

Terrah shrugged. "Well, you *did* make me a promise."

He pressed her even closer to him. "Oh, and what did I promise?"

"On the plane, you promised to make me say your name over and over again."

She drew in a deep breath against his chest, loving the smell of his skin mingled with traces of her body oil. "I only said it *once.*"

Nick gave her a dark grin that made her stomach flip.

"Actually, you said my name twice."

Terrah held up her finger and wagged it. "*But* only once 'on the edge of a scream'. And that *is* what you promised...or have you forgotten?"

"No, and you won't ever forget it, either, when it happens again."

He ground his hips against her and she believed him. How could she want him so badly again?

"Don't you worry, babe" — Nick nipped her neck with his teeth, sending erotic shivers down her spine — "I *always* make good on my promises." He searched her face for a moment. "No regrets?"

There it was...the question she'd been avoiding asking herself since they'd got out of bed.

"Terrah?"

She rubbed her hand on his rock-hard chest and smiled up at him. "Regret all this? No way."

Nick laughed as he squeezed her ass. "Good...because we're just getting started," he said. He released her and stepped into the shower.

She stared at him through the steamed glass door as he lathered his chest, and had to literally force herself to pivot and walk towards the bathroom door.

"Oh, and Terrah?"

She glanced back to him, her gaze following the trail of bubbles racing down his pecs and ripped abs.

"Don't wear any panties while we're here together on the island."

There were no words for what that demanding statement did to her equilibrium.

Nick winked before turning his back on her.

She left him lathering beneath the streaming water, wishing she could scrub her own mind free of her thoughts. Her response to Nick's question had been true. She didn't have any regrets about sleeping with him—being with Nick had been one of the most erotic experiences in her life. Yet a part of her wondered what she'd just got herself into. She didn't engage in sexual flings, but here she was, involved in one.

Can you handle it?

"I'm a big girl."

Terrah tossed her towel on the bed, ignored her bra and picked her dress up off the floor by the foot of the bed. She could handle a tropical fling with a hot model. A little fun in the sun was exactly what she needed...*deserved,* after the sexual drought she'd emerged from.

Terrah pulled on her dress. She wouldn't be foolish enough to let her heart get involved. Terrah scoffed as she slipped the straps of her dress over her shoulders. That wouldn't even be possible in the short time they'd be on the island.

The sound of light knocking on the door saved her from thinking about it any further. She wrenched her dress into place as Nick came out of the bathroom with only a towel cinched around his waist.

"I'll get it."

The bellhop wheeled in their brunch, not even blinking an eye at his state of undress. Sweet scents of cinnamon and bacon filled the air and Terrah's stomach rumbled.

"Do you want to eat on the deck?" Nick asked, after tipping the bellboy and closing the door.

"Sounds goo—" She paused, momentarily distracted as his towel fell to the floor and he proceeded to put on his linen pants, commando-style. "Sounds good."

He grinned at her. "Let's eat."

"Aren't you going to put on a shirt?"

"Will it be too distracting for you if I don't?"

Terrah rolled her eyes. "Please, I see hot bodies all day long."

"Right," Nick said as he put on his T-shirt, giving Terrah plenty of time to appreciate his washboard abs.

She was playing it cool, but Nick, in any state of undress, distracted her to hell.

Terrah slipped back into her heels, then rushed forward to open the glass doors leading out to the deck. Nick pushed the trolley containing their food forward and inhaled the sultry breeze that washed over them when they stepped outside. The sun was fading already, leaving swirls of red and orange across the sky, and Terrah was captivated by the beauty of the island. She looked over the balcony railing to see the pool shimmering bright blue and, farther out, she could see the ocean. She took in a deep breath and smiled.

I'm in Hawaii with the man of my erotic dreams!

She closed her eyes for a moment, just listening to the wind and the faint laugher and music drifting up from the poolside.

"It's so beautiful here."

"I know. You haven't even seen the prettiest parts of the island. Mimosa?"

"Yes, please." Terrah sat down as Nick placed their dishes on the wooden table. "Mmm… Breakfast is my favourite meal."

"I told you I knew what you wanted."

They had Belgian waffles topped with whipped cream and sliced mangoes, two thick pieces of bacon and scrambled eggs topped with Cheddar cheese.

Terrah took a bite of her waffles and moaned with pleasure. "This is so good. Wait until I tell my sister about this mango topping."

"Mango is good on so many things." Nick pointed his fork in her direction. "It's nice to be with a woman who can appreciate good food."

"The usual model types you date stick to carrots and coffee, eh?"

"How did you know?" He gave her a mock-shocked expression as she laughed.

"I'm not exaggerating."

He bit into his bacon as he shook his head. "Oh, I *know* you aren't."

"I gave up on being model-thin a long time ago."

"Thank God. I don't understand why women don't embrace what makes them feminine in a man's eyes. I like to *feel* the curves of the woman I'm with."

Terrah's eyes dropped to his lips as he lifted a forkful of eggs to his mouth. "I can tell."

"I love touching your body."

"I love the *way* you touch my body."

Whoa!

Something about Nick made her comfortable enough to simply say what was on her mind. Heat rushed to her cheeks as she bit into a slice of mango. The sweet, juicy flavour exploded on her tongue as she licked the whipped cream on her bottom lip and held Nick's gaze.

"Not half as much as I do."

Nick watched Terrah lick off the sweet cream on her lip and was instantly aroused. She was easily the sexiest female he'd ever seen, including all the models he'd ever worked with. He enjoyed talking to her. There was nothing pretentious or demanding about her personality. He liked the way she laughed and moaned as he caressed her. And he absolutely fucking *loved* the way she felt around his cock.

Hell, you just like everything about her.

Yeah.

Like the way he could read her emotions so easily in the warm depths of her eyes. He knew she was embarrassed by what she'd just told him, and he found her shyness endearing. His eyes travelled down the length of her leg to the red heels he'd noticed the moment he'd opened the door.

"I want to touch you now."

"You haven't finished your breakfast." Her voice was teasing, but he could see the flare of passion sparking in her honey-brown eyes.

"Give me your foot."

Her eyes widened as she took another bite of waffle covered with whipped cream and mango. He waited for her to ask why or to hesitate, but she complied, placing her red heel onto his knee.

"This is a gorgeous shoe."

Nick stroked her ankle as he stared down at her perfectly painted toes, showcased in the elegant heel.

"Thank you. I saw these and had to have them. They were an extravagant indulgence."

"You should have lots of those." He gently removed the shoe and set it on the cement floor. "Such pretty toes. Are you ticklish?"

"Yes!"

Nick dipped his index finger into the leftover whipped cream on his plate, then dripped a little over Terrah's toes.

"Nick!"

"I wanted to do this to you the first time I held your foot in my hand."

He shifted his chair closer to her as he lifted her foot to his mouth and ran his tongue over the top of her toes. Holding her gaze, he sucked and licked every bit of the cream off.

"Did that make you wanna laugh?" His voice was husky, and he could see her breathing faster as she shook her head. "What does it do?"

He kissed the arch of her foot and the hemline of her sundress inched up, exposing her luscious thighs.

"Makes me wet."

"Show me."

Nick could see the rapidly beating pulse at the base of Terrah's neck as she glanced around at the empty balconies on either side of them. It appeared there was no one above or below them, which gave the illusion of privacy.

"Someone might see."

He could hear the nervousness in her voice, but the excitement sparkling in her eyes made him press her harder. "Show me, Terrah."

Nick placed her bare foot on his leg and settled back in his chair. He saw her gaze shift to his semi-erect cock, pressed against the soft fabric of his linen pants.

"You can see how much I want you. It's only fair for me to see you, too."

"Hardly fair," she said with a smirk.

His eyes dropped to her breasts. She'd gone braless and he could see the faint outline of her nipples as she crossed her arms.

"Stop stalling and show me that wet pussy."

That seemed to push her past any fears. Terrah released her arms to grip the edge of the chair while

Nick kept his eyes on her face. Something wild flashed in her eyes and then she slowly parted her legs. She inched the bottom of her dress up to mid thigh and his cock stirred.

Nick dropped his gaze to Terrah's partially revealed pussy and shook his head. "I can't see, Terrah."

"Come on!"

It felt as if all the blood in his body rushed to his cock at the sound of the breathless desperation in her voice.

Nick met her eyes. "Wider."

Terrah hesitated for a moment. He resisted the urge to kiss her as she caught her bottom lip between her teeth and exhaled.

"Show me."

Rock hard now, Nick watched her scoot her bottom down a little further in her chair. She leaned all the way back and parted her thighs. Nick drank in the vision of her, wet and exposed to him, before she shifted her position.

"I *know* you saw that."

"I did, but I'm not satisfied."

Terrah lifted one eyebrow. "No?"

"No. Come here."

Plant leaves flapped in the gentle wind sweeping over the balcony as Nick waited to see what Terrah would do.

He didn't have to wait long.

She slipped her foot out of her other heel, got up from her chair and took a step towards him. He grabbed her by the waist, pushed his knees between her legs and encouraged her to straddle him. She sat down on his lap and he placed his mouth around one protruding nipple through the soft fabric of her sundress.

"Nick, this is crazy."

He sucked harder, pulling on her nipple with his teeth as he scooted her bare bottom tight against his erection. The straps to her sundress fell down from her shoulders and he pressed his lips there, loving the smell of her skin. He nipped her with his teeth as she slipped one of her hands between them.

"Do you want to stop?" He whispered the words against her lips as she touched his cock and he slid one finger over her clit.

"No fair...no fair," she moaned as he caressed her.

"You're so wet, Terrah."

She kissed him while she untied the drawstring on his baggy linen pants and freed his cock. Nick sucked in a tight breath as she wrapped her hand around him.

"I want you inside of me."

Hearing those six breathy words did something to him. His hand slipped from her slick heat as he reached into his pocket to extract a condom. He tore it open, sheathing himself as Terrah lifted up off his lap slightly, ready to take him in.

"Put me inside of you."

Terrah took him in her hand again, guiding the crown of his cock to her slick entrance. He watched her bite her lip as she slowly lowered herself onto his lap.

"Mmm..."

Her throaty sounds of pleasure heightened his enjoyment. He ground his teeth as her silky heat hugged his cock in a sweet, tight hold. Slipping his hands under her thighs, he helped steady her as she took him deep within her.

"Feels so good."

'Good' didn't begin to describe it as she gently rocked her hips. She placed her hands on his shoulders and, with subtle movements, began creating a delicious friction that made him grit his teeth. He forced himself to remain still, letting her set the pace, but her moans of bliss and the feel of her, so wet and snug around him, made it difficult.

"I need more." Terrah's voice was a ragged whisper against his ear.

Thank God.

He was dying a slow, erotic death with her easy riding.

"Hold on to my pants and wrap your arms around my neck."

Terrah locked her legs behind his back as he got up from the chair. She tightened her sheath around his cock, which only fuelled his need to get her back inside. Nick pushed open the sliding door and carried her to the dining table, only a few steps away. He sat Terrah down on the edge of the table. His pants fell to the floor and Nick stepped out of them as she lay back. She looked beautiful in the gentle light filtering into the room from the bathroom.

Terrah beckoned to him. "Now give it to me hard."

Nick groaned at the feel of her drenched pussy tightening around his cock. He dragged the front of her dress down with one hand, exposing her breasts. She bit her lip and moaned when he tweaked one beaded nipple with his fingers. He loved the tiny gasp that escaped her lips as he slipped his hands under her knees and yanked her ass just a little way off the table. Never had he seen a more luscious sight than Terrah all sprawled out before him, hungrily waiting for him.

He placed her legs over his shoulders and the position gave him maximum penetration. Nick began thrusting into her and Terrah's delighted whimpers were music to his ears. He pumped her deeper and watched her eyes flutter closed with each measured stroke. "Is this what you want, Terrah?"

Her lips parted in silent moans of ecstasy as he worked his cock in and out of her juicy pussy.

"Yes, oh, yes!"

He fucked her even harder, determined to give her exactly what she needed...what *he* needed. The faster he sank into her softness, the more he was certain he'd always want *more*. He lost track of her cries and his thrusts as that one word rang in his head with every piston movement of his hips.

More... More... More of...

"Terrah..."

Chapter Eleven

Terrah screamed as she came, breaking apart into a million shards of pure sensory bliss. She called out his name as he'd called hers, delirious with pleasure. Her heartbeat roared in her ears as she gripped the sides of the table, trembling and gasping for air. Her eyelids fluttered open to see Nick's eyes closed, his gorgeous profile glistening with sweat. His hands tightened on her calves for a moment before he took her legs from his shoulders. She whimpered as he slid his hands under her knees, spread her legs wide and thrust into her at a frenzied pace.

The friction of his cock inside her after climaxing was almost too intense. She uttered sounds she'd never made before as Nick found his own release with a gruff groan. Nick rocked the table and Terrah could feel the rhythmic pulse of his orgasm vibrating within her.

Nick kissed her knee and Terrah moaned when he slipped from her body. He moved to her side and she pressed her sticky thighs together with a lazy smile as he moved to her side and brushed his lips against hers.

"*That*" — she sucked in a ragged breath — "was amazing."

"Incredible."

She held out her hands and he took them, pulling her up into a sitting position. "*Delicious.*"

"*You*" — he kissed her hard on the lips as he let go of her hands — "are delicious."

Terrah thought he looked delectable with his dark hair sticking to his sweaty brow. She was certain he could sell a billion magazines with the way he looked right now, especially with the searing look of passion still burning in his blue-green eyes.

Terrah lifted the top of her sundress back up over her breasts and inched off the table. She had tiny aches in places she'd never noticed before. She felt wonderfully sated and naughty.

Nick brought that out in her and she liked it — a lot.

"Spend the rest of the day with me. We'll get up in the morning and go to the shoot together."

He flipped on the light over the table, zipped and tied his pants before his eyes locked with hers.

Gorgeous, make-you-wanna-melt eyes.

She wanted to stay. It was on the tip of her tongue to just say yes, but she needed some time to sort out all the weird emotions crowding her thoughts right now. Plus, she needed a good night's rest if she wanted to be on top of her game tomorrow. Staying the night would ensure neither one of them got any sleep.

"Terrah, what do you say?"

"It's very tempting, but..."

"But...?"

He came to her, wrapped his arms around her waist.

"But...I think I should go back to my room."

Nick studied her face for a second. "Are you sure?"

Terrah nodded. "I'm afraid, if I stay the night, we won't get much sleep and Aidan will know we are both not at one hundred per cent. You know he'll notice."

Nick nodded as he released her. "I can't even tempt you to shower with me before you go?"

"Next time, remember?"

"Don't *you* forget."

"I won't." Terrah grabbed her purse off the nightstand. "I need my shoes."

"I'll get them."

She was at the door when he presented her with her red heels. Terrah laughed when he got down on one knee and looked up at her.

"May I have your left foot, please?"

She obliged, biting her lip as Nick kissed her toes and slipped on the heel. He was easily the most sensual man she'd ever been with.

"May I have your *right* foot, please?"

Terrah ruffled his thick hair and a whorl of emotions wrapped around her heart when he gave the other foot the exact same treatment. Emotionally and physically tired, she smiled at Nick, ready to escape back to reality.

"Thank you."

He stood up and his eyes held hers while one corner of his mouth lifted in amusement.

"My pleasure."

He dipped his head and kissed her, slowly and tenderly. Terrah clung to him, loving the way his hands gripped her waist. She felt as if he'd imprinted his taste on her forever. He pulled away and she found it hard to find the doorknob that was only inches away from her hand.

"I enjoyed brunch, Nick."

He flashed her a sexy grin and heat rose to her cheeks.

Of all the things to say, she'd had to mention food?

Terrah felt like an idiot. Her mind was a slurry of conflicting voices as she fumbled and finally found the doorknob.

Turn the knob. C'mon, Terrah.

With what seemed like extreme effort, she twisted the cool metal in her hand and opened the door. She stepped into the hall and lifted her chin to meet Nick's eyes as he leaned against the door. His gaze travelled over her lips for a brief second, making her stomach dip.

"I enjoyed brunch, too, Terrah. See you in the morning."

"Later."

She turned around and walked away, conscious of her wet thighs and Nick still watching her from his doorway. When she heard his door click closed she exhaled, replaying every intimate moment between them as she practically floated down the hall. Nick was an amazing lover.

He's amazing, period.

Funny, engaging, romantic...*sexy.*

"Can't forget sexy," Terrah muttered as she approached her door and pulled out her key card.

She was beginning to wonder if she'd become involved in something she had no way of controlling. In less than thirty-six hours, Nick had completely turned her world upside down. She'd told herself she'd indulge in a hot fling with him, but maybe she couldn't handle the smouldering heat. Nick kept surprising her. He was nothing like the man she'd assumed him to be.

Terrah placed her electronic key in the door, smiling as she thought about his kisses on the plane. He'd helped her get over her anxiety with his unconventional, but totally effective method. Her Hawaiian trip was turning out to be interesting for reasons she hadn't even anticipated.

"Terrah?"

She turned around and found Jocelyn staring at her in astonishment, with Lyn Lee, another model, standing beside her.

Great.

"I assume you're here to make us look gorgeous for tomorrow's shoot?" Jocelyn tossed her bone-straight blonde tresses over her shoulder.

Terrah opened her mouth to respond as Jocelyn turned away to continue talking to Lyn.

"Aidan Marks liked the proofs with Nick and me so much, he personally asked me to join this shoot here in Hawaii!"

"I'm excited to be working with him on this, too," Lyn said, looking at Terrah. "Hi, I'm Lyn Lee."

The beautiful Asian model held out her hand and Terrah shook it with a warm smile.

"Nice to officially meet you, Lyn. I look forward to working with you both tomorrow."

"Did you just arrive?"

"Um, a few hours ago," Terrah answered, mentally selecting which eyeshadow colours she wanted to try on Lyn in the morning.

Jocelyn sighed. "I wish I'd gotten here earlier. My agent had to juggle another shoot for this, but I pleaded with her to do whatever it took to get me here. I wanted to visit the islands again before the year was up." Jocelyn tugged up the bodice of her strapless fuchsia mini dress as Lyn and Terrah looked at her.

"Wait until you see Nick. His photos don't do him justice."

Lyn smiled. "I believe you."

"The photos from our last shoot together were incredible."

"I can't wait to see how they turned out."

Jocelyn gave Terrah a bright smile. "They're *fabulous*. I'm so looking forward to working with *him* again."

Isn't this awkward?

"Well, I'll see you guys in the morning."

"Later, Terrah," Lyn said with a grin as she glanced at Jocelyn. "I suppose we should do something low key, so we can be up at the crack of dawn."

Jocelyn offered a small wave as the two models continued walking down the hall. Terrah fumbled to get her key in the door. She could hear Jocelyn as she continued to talk about Nick to Lyn.

"I'm right across the hall from Nick. I'm going to have to resist knocking on his door to say hello."

Terrah could hear Lyn giggle as she opened her door. She stepped inside her room and kicked off her heels, suddenly exhausted.

Right across the hall?

How convenient.

"Stop."

With a weary sigh, Terrah shook her head as she stripped out of her dress and headed towards the bathroom. She refused to indulge the cynical thoughts racing in her head. Until she saw reason to believe otherwise...she was going to take Nick at his word.

He wasn't interested in Jocelyn.

Terrah stared at her reflection in the mirror and faced a cold, hard fact.

It bothered her. Jocelyn across the hall from Nick's room bothered the hell out of her, which was ridiculous. She knew exactly what a fling was and what it was not…or, at least, in theory.

Sleep… She needed to sleep.

One thing was for sure, Jocelyn would pursue Nick. Blondie would never believe he wasn't into her.

Things were definitely going to be interesting at tomorrow's shoot.

* * * *

Terrah snatched her sunglasses off the top of her head and put them on. It was just after eleven in the morning and the sun was shining brightly, setting off the iridescent sequins on Jocelyn's shimmering, skin-tight, full body leotard. Strategically placed beading concealed her nakedness, but the sheer outfit left nothing to the imagination. Terrah had curled her blonde hair so that it cascaded around her shoulders, the perfect complement to her ethereal makeup. She truly resembled a goddess as she lay on a stone bench, which had been placed in the sand so the ocean washed ashore behind her.

Lyn Lee was gorgeous beneath the sun, kneeling in front of Jocelyn in a lupine pose. Her dark, straight hair nearly touched the sand. Her smoky eyes looked flawless and Terrah was certain she'd done some of her best work on Lyn. The models were surrounded by lush foliage winding around the fake Greek columns. It was the ultimate backdrop, especially with Nick as the focal point.

"More. I want to *feel* how much you want him, ladies," Aidan called out as he snapped frame after frame. "That's it. It's all in the eyes. Touch his leg, Jocelyn."

Terrah watched Jocelyn run her hand down Nick's thigh. As she wrapped her small hand around his calf muscle, the lithe model gazed up at him with a look of utter adoration and longing that Terrah was certain wasn't just an act for the camera.

A flash of jealousy momentarily took her by surprise. She drew in a deep breath, exhaled slowly, mentally pushing the unwanted feeling away.

You are not going there, Terrah.

They'd spent one afternoon together...one incredible, mind-blowing afternoon.

She wasn't about to confuse good sex with something more. The green-eyed monster was *not* going to get the best of her.

Aidan moved in front of her, directing a different pose for Lyn as Terrah's gaze fell back on Nick. He looked incredible standing between the women, dressed in a white toga that showcased his muscled arms, chest and legs. Around his head he wore the classic laurel wreath. He had one hand on his hip and the other outstretched to the heavens, with the bottle of cologne the whole shoot was centred on balanced on his palm.

"That's it... Worship the ground he stands on."

The marketing campaign for the popular fragrance was brilliant. *Smell like a man. Be worshipped like a god.*

"I'd worship him with or without the cologne. He is so yummy!"

You have no idea. Terrah gave Ginny a small smile, wishing the production assistant were still on her mini smoking break.

"C'mon, tell me you don't agree."

"I agree."

Ginny grinned, tossing her over-processed blonde hair back. "I love the makeup you did, Terrah. I've been meaning to ask whether you do private consultations."

"Not as much as I used to."

Ginny nodded. "I bet you could make any woman look beautiful."

"I'd like to think so."

Ginny turned her attention back to the modelling shoot with a wistful look on her face.

Terrah could almost feel how badly Ginny wanted to be in front of the camera. The production assistant had shared with her once how she'd tried to break into the modelling business in her teens. Ginny was what many in the industry referred to as a model wannabe, getting as close to the modelling world as she could with her job and lifestyle.

"After this ad goes live, *every* man will want to wear that cologne. Have you smelled it yet?"

"Not yet."

Ginny gasped in mock horror as she whipped a small vial from her pocket. "I snatched a few samples from the promo table."

Terrah took the sample, popped off the lid and sniffed the fragrance. "Mmm…this is nice."

"Isn't it? I wonder if Nick Tasso wears it."

"He doesn't."

She didn't have to turn her head to know Ginny was staring at her. Terrah tore her eyes off Nick to see the quizzical look on Ginny's face. A rush of heat raced up her back as she cleared her throat.

"I didn't smell it on him when I was doing his makeup earlier."

Or when he pushed me onto the bed and…

Terrah snapped the lid back on the vial and handed it back to the production assistant. Her cheeks felt hot as she tried to clear the erotic images of her tryst with

Nick from her mind. Moisture dampened her panties, her body responding to memories of his touch as if his hands were on her right now.

"Well, he doesn't need anything more adding to his sex appeal anyway. He's already lethal to us ladies." Ginny giggled as she pocketed the cologne sample.

"Terrah?"

Terrah glanced over Ginny's shoulder at the sound of Aidan's voice, and saw him beckoning for her to come closer. She went to him, grateful for the distraction.

"Can you tease Jocelyn's hair like we discussed for the final pose?" Aidan asked, barely glancing at her as he fiddled with his camera.

"I'm on it."

She turned away from Aidan and her eyes locked with Nick's. Her heartbeat tripled. No way was she imagining the hunger...no, the *eroticism* in his level gaze. Nipple-tightening arcs of desire wound through her as his aqua green eyes swept over her. She wished the two of them were alone so he could take away the longing that was driving her to distraction.

A salty breeze rifled her skirt, teased the wet cotton between her legs and reminded Terrah of Nick's naughty request that she not wear any panties while on the island. She'd been unwilling to comply once she'd got dressed and considered the possibility of someone else discovering her lack of underwear while at the shoot. Terrah didn't regret her decision, the way the wind was pushing up her skirt.

Terrah cursed under her breath. Her physical reaction to Nick embarrassed and surprised her. She'd never soaked her panties this fast over the mere thought of a man.

She moved forward, conscious of the warm sand beneath her bare feet and the heat of Nick's gaze on her as she came closer. Terrah was grateful he couldn't see her eyes behind her dark shades. She was certain he'd know instantly just how much she wanted to have him...*again.*

Nick watched Terrah approach, captivated by the rhythm and sensuality of her walk. She moved with a natural grace and sexiness that would give any model he knew a run for their money. His gaze ran up her bare feet to her skirt swirling around her legs and he wondered if she'd adhered to his request and gone pantyless. Just the thought of her bare beneath her clothing made him want to go to her. He wished he could see her eyes behind those Hollywood shades she was wearing.

Did she want him again as much as he wanted her?

He couldn't wait to have her all to himself. They'd have dinner together. Take a walk on the beach. The whole night would be theirs. Being with Terrah had been the most enjoyable time he'd spent with a woman in a while.

Jocelyn squeezed his leg as Nick gritted his teeth.

He couldn't wait to get away from her. She wanted to talk with him about something important after the shoot, but as far as he was concerned there was nothing left to say. Her not-so-subtle flirtations were beginning to really annoy him, and if she mentioned one more time 'how incredible they looked together', he'd personally drag her into the ocean and dunk her beneath the rolling waves.

Nick smiled, imagining the prissy model flapping in the water, wet and horrified.

Mmm...wet.

His thoughts turned back to Terrah. She'd been so responsive to his touch yesterday, so wet around his cock. All morning long he'd been thinking about how good it had felt kissing and holding her body. She had the sexiest laugh, especially when it was husky with desire. She was the kind of lover a man hoped for—adventurous and insatiable.

Great.

He'd managed to keep his lustful thoughts under control...until now.

What would everyone say if he just snaked out his arm, grabbed Terrah and kissed her?

Tabloid news, for sure.

He was certain Terrah wouldn't appreciate such a grandstand move. She was all about professionalism, and so was he.

Yeah, so why are you thinking about going all caveman-style and kissing her in front of all these people?

Good question.

Maybe to prove to her once and for all how much he was into her. Terrah still had lingering doubts about that. He could see it in her eyes even after they'd been intimate. God, how could she have any doubts after the passion they'd shared?

Chapter Twelve

Nick shifted his weight as Terrah fussed with Jocelyn's hair, his eyes drawn to the full swell of Terrah's breasts in the soft material of her blouse. He could just make out the faint outline of each tight bud. Her nipples were hard and he knew exactly how sensitive they were...how she'd arched her back when he'd flicked them with his thumb.

Nick remembered how Terrah had writhed beneath him when he'd tongued the tips of her breasts, and blood rushed to his cock.

Think about anything else but sex.

It wasn't uncommon for male models to get hard when working with their female counterparts, but Nick couldn't remember the last time that had happened to him. Sporting wood would raise eyebrows and tongues would definitely wag, especially since Jocelyn was involved in the photo shoot.

Too late.

He was in trouble. His cock had a mind of its own.

Nick shifted his weight, hoping to send the surge of blood past the centre of his body and to any other muscle group.

Stop looking at her breasts, man.

With concentrated effort, he dragged his eyes upward to the elegant column of Terrah's neck. She'd smelled so damn good when he'd kissed her there.

"Looking good, Terrah," Aidan called from behind a camera.

Indeed, Nick thought as she stopped mussing with Jocelyn's ridiculously curly locks. He thought he could feel her eyes on him before she turned around and walked away.

The edge of the skirt she was wearing flitted in the wind, and Nick stared at the ample curve of her bottom as she padded across the sand barefoot.

He loved her ass.

Was she bare and wet for him?

The need to know was killing him.

"This is it, gang—give me all you got."

Jocelyn squeezed his calf muscle again as Aidan resumed shooting.

Stay focused.

He was focused…focused on every erotic moment he had shared with Terrah. The scent of her skin. The feel of her so warm and snug around his cock distracted him, but it was the memory of her moans of pleasure as he took them both over the edge that made his dick swell unrelentingly, heedless of his mental commands.

Damn!

He couldn't chance moving and messing up his position. Hopefully the layered cotton material of his toga would provide some coverage.

Nick stole a glance downward between shots and saw Jocelyn staring at his hard-on, enjoying her bird's-eye view. Her hand tightened on his leg and Nick could hear her almost inaudible sigh of delight.

It's not for you, sweet tart.

Jocelyn caught his eye and had the good grace to blush before averting her attention elsewhere.

Yeah, no way the toga was going to hide his full-fledged erection.

It looked like he was going to be the talk of the shoot, after all.

"Oh, my, my, my…"

"What?" Terrah glanced up from the text she was sending her sister to see Ginny's attention transfixed on the models.

"It looks like Jocelyn's finally getting a *rise* outta Nick."

Terrah turned to look at Nick as Ginny giggled. Her stomach did that weird flip she was now accustomed to feeling around him. Her eyes ran over his muscled body, to settle on the unmistakable bulge of his cock barely concealed by the material of his toga.

"Can you imagine all *that* being for you?" Ginny bit into a carrot stick with a wistful look. "Jocelyn's so lucky."

Irritation almost prompted Terrah to say she didn't have to imagine it, but she bit her tongue and tried to ignore the hateful green-eyed monster whispering in her ear as she stared at Jocelyn's hand, which had risen even higher on Nick's thigh. The heightened colour on the model's cheeks had nothing to do with Terrah's makeup job.

"And that's a wrap, people, thank you."

A round of applause broke out when Aidan handed his camera to one assistant and took the mimosa offered to him by another. He lifted his glass and a cheer went up as the models finally relaxed. Someone turned up the radio, blasting local music, and the noise level increased.

Terrah watched Nick help Jocelyn up from the sand before forcing herself to focus on loading up her makeup. She was hungry and tired. Sleep hadn't come easy last night. It felt like she had tossed and turned the whole time, thinking about Nick. She was going to pack up, get back to her room and read on her balcony with a mimosa of her own.

"Are you going to Aidan's luau later?" Ginny asked, still chomping on carrot sticks. "It's gonna be wild!"

"I don't know." Terrah closed the lid on her case. She knew how *wild* Aidan's parties could get.

"Well, hopefully I'll see you tonight. Enjoy the rest of your time on the island."

"Thanks, Ginny — you, too."

The production assistant smiled at her as she stuffed the bag of carrots back into her shoulder bag. She pulled out a box of cigarettes and walked away as Terrah's phone rang.

"Hello?"

"You broke your cardinal rule, eh?"

"Hey, Audrey." Terrah plugged one ear to hear her sister chuckling. "Don't laugh."

"What? That text was funny. So which rule are you talking about? You know you have more than one."

Terrah laughed. "I'm talking about the only one I *haven't* broken."

"Ummm… Yeah, I still don't know which one you're talking about."

"I went out with one of the models I work with."

"Really? Which one? Don't tell me it's that dark chocolate hottie from Jamaica. Ooh, la la!"

"No, not him, and it isn't *who* that matters, but *what* am I going to do now that does."

"You're leaving out some serious details in this story."

"Audrey, I don't have time to share details."

"Okay, I'll fill them in. You went out with this gorgeous mystery model, had sex — really good sex, which is so unlike you — and now you're a-*dick*-ted to something you're afraid you can't really have because he's a famous model. How'd I do?"

Terrah closed her eyes and exhaled.

"Hello?"

"I'm here." Terrah opened her eyes and noticed Nick and the other models were gone.

"Is this guy a womanising jerk?"

"No...I don't think so."

"Was it a one-night stand?"

"One *afternoon*, remember?"

"Well, did he push you outta bed the moment he came?"

Terrah laughed. "No, he didn't, Audrey. I went back to my room."

"Did it seem like he wanted you to stay?"

Terrah thought about Nick kissing her feet as he helped her put on her shoes and smiled. "He asked me to, but I turned him down."

"Well, I think you should stop overthinking, get off the phone and see what happens next."

"See what happens next..."

Terrah watched the production crew begin to dismantle the Greek columns. Little by little, they dragged the foliage away, eventually leaving the beach clear.

"You never know what could happen if you're open to all the possibilities."

"Since when did you become so optimistic?" Terrah teased, waving to Michelle, who she'd barely had a chance to say two words to during the entire shoot.

Audrey squealed. "Since Derek proposed!"

"Wait—what? He proposed?" Terrah dropped her case on the sand. "You let me go on and on about nothing with this kinda news to share?"

"It happened last night—he totally surprised me. Can you believe it?" Audrey's voice wobbled.

"Oh, I'm so happy for you guys. Congratulations!"

"Go on and say it…"

"Say what?"

"It was about time."

Terrah grinned as Audrey blew her nose. She could picture the happy tears falling down her sister's face. "Everything happens when it's supposed to happen."

Audrey giggled. "Now who sounds optimistic?"

"Hey, your good news has inspired me."

"Good! I love you."

"Love you back."

Terrah ended the call, staring out at the ocean in a daze. Her little sister was getting married. Audrey had found the right man who wanted to take their committed relationship to the ultimate level. Terrah was happy Audrey's life was coming together, but wished she had some clear direction in her own when it came to love. She couldn't even figure out how to handle a hot island fling.

"Another beautiful job done here today, Terrah."

Terrah whipped around to see Michelle smiling at her. The art director handed her the second mimosa in her hand.

"I loved doing this shoot." Terrah reached for the drink and took a sip. "Mmm...thanks for this, too."

"You're welcome. I do believe this is the best mimosa I've ever had."

"It's delicious." Terrah reached for her case and followed Michelle back through the sand towards the main road, where the rest of the crew was still loading up.

Where is Nick?

"I wondered about the chemistry translating on film with the models today, but Jocelyn and Nick really cranked up the heat."

"I'm sure Aidan got some super-sexy shots."

"Oh, he did." Michelle cleared her throat. "Those three were whisked away to shower and change before the promotional luncheon for the ad campaign. I just hope they stay long enough to satisfy the cologne ad execs that flew in some top-notch investors to wine, dine and impress."

Terrah set her glass on a table alongside Michelle's, mentally pushing back her disappointment. She wouldn't be seeing Nick anytime soon.

Michelle stifled a yawn. "I just want to take a nap. My flight leaves in about nine hours. I need to get back for another client."

"Oh, wow, you deserve a nap."

"I'm going to sleep on the plane. We better hurry or we're going to miss the shuttle taking us back to the hotel," Michelle said, picking up the pace towards the shuttle bus. Music was blasting from the vehicle almost as loudly as the rambunctious laughter.

The last thing Terrah wanted to do was get on that bus.

"Terrah!"

She turned her head to see Aidan approaching with more mimosas in both hands, all smiles now that the shoot was over. He looked like an island local, dressed in cut-off jeans and a light blue Hawaiian shirt.

"Share a toast with me, ladies?"

Michelle beamed at the invitation as she shook her head. "I'd love to, but I've gotta get back. Aidan, it was a pleasure working with you today."

"Likewise."

Photographer and art director exchanged a light hug before Michelle turned to her.

"I'm sure I'll be talking to you next week. *Aloha*."

"*Aloha*," Terrah and Aidan echoed, watching the art director board the shuttle.

Terrah pushed her shades up into her hair as Aidan focused his full attention on her.

"What about you? Are you ready to go back, or can I persuade you to have a toast with me in celebration of another fantastic shoot?"

"It's a long walk back to the hotel from here."

Aidan grinned. "I've got a car that'll get you there without breaking a sweat."

She didn't have any other plans and, at the very least, sharing a toast with Aidan would allow her to skip out on the crowded shuttle ride.

Why not?

Terrah took the mimosa from his hand. "To what shall we toast?"

"To beauty."

The shuttle bus with the rest of the crew pulled off as she lifted her glass.

"To beauty."

Aidan reached up, touched her fingers grasping the glass, stopping her from bringing it to her lips.

"To *your* beauty."

"Oh, wow, thank you." Terrah smiled brightly at Aidan's revised toast, ignoring the flirtatious smile on his lips as she pulled her hand from his and took a sip from her glass.

"I'm glad you decided to join me for a drink. Now, why don't you join me for dinner tonight?" Aidan glanced at his watch. "You *did* promise me a dinner date."

"What about the party you're throwing this evening?"

Aidan tilted his head back with a chuckle. "Right. I made those plans on a whim, but I'd happily change them to spend the evening with you."

"I think a lot of people would be disappointed."

"I don't care."

Terrah knew he'd cancel the luau in a flash if she gave him the green light. She averted her eyes from his handsome face, drawing a line in the sand with her toe.

"Aidan…"

"Don't say it. I can read the no in your eyes."

She met his gaze again. "I'm always open to dinner with friends."

"Ouch." Aidan downed the contents of his glass. "You've just dashed all my hopes of sweeping you off your feet all over again in a whirlwind romance."

Terrah laughed. "I'm sorry."

"Sure, you are," Aidan said, chuckling with her.

"Seriously, Aidan, I'm really glad I got to work with you again."

Aidan waved his hand. "You're talented as hell. I hope to use you again in the future."

"Anytime," Terrah said, pleased by his words. She dropped her gaze to the blowing sand around her toes as Aidan stared at her. "I look forward to the creative challenge."

"You know...you're even sexier now than you were when we first met."

Terrah flushed under his intense stare. "Why, thank you, Aidan."

Aidan laughed. "And a whole lot more confident. I can see that in your work and in you."

"Experience will give that to you. I've been lucky to snag the right jobs and make the right contacts."

"Your career is just getting started. I know you are going to go far in this business." Aidan glanced at his watch. "Well, if we can't do dinner, let me take you to lunch."

"Um..."

"I insist. C'mon, it's only lunch."

He held out his hand with a devilish grin.

"Okay, lunch it is." Terrah took his hand and they started walking up the few steps leading up out of the sand to the road, where a fancy sports car convertible awaited them. Aidan opened the door, and she dusted her feet before sliding into the leather seat with an inward sigh.

"You are going to love this restaurant."

Aidan closed her door, running around to his own as she slipped on her sandals. He was obviously very pleased she'd agreed to lunch. He was always happy when things went his way. Terrah exhaled, wondering how Nick was enjoying the luncheon as Aidan got into the car.

Was he thinking about her as much as she was thinking about him?

"Today's shoot went even better than I imagined. I love it when I can easily get the pictures I want with the models."

Terrah stared out at the ocean as Aidan started chatting about all the sexy shots he'd captured, especially between Nick and Jocelyn. He was content to talk shop now that he knew where he stood with her romantically. Terrah nodded at something he'd said, her mind a million miles away. She wished she were already back at the hotel.

Terrah glanced at Aidan animatedly moving his free hand as he talked, oblivious to her lacklustre responses. He was still the same charming, talented, self-absorbed man she remembered. The salty wind rushing through the convertible drowned out his voice as she stifled a yawn.

I should've got on the damn shuttle.

Chapter Thirteen

"After you," Aidan said, holding the door open for her.

"Thank you."

They walked into the upscale restaurant and tempting scents wafted over Terrah.

"Mr Marks, your table is this way."

Terrah returned the waiter's warm smile and ignored the irritation she felt when Aidan placed his hand on the small of her back. She gritted her teeth as he guided them after their waiter through the crowded restaurant and focused instead on the beauty of the space they were about to dine in. Huge, leafy green plants created secluded areas, a pianist played familiar tunes and open patio doors brought in warm breezes off the ocean. The place was filled with patrons enjoying themselves.

"They have coconut lobster skewers here that will make you never want to leave this island."

"I bet."

Terrah looked away from Aidan as they continued to walk through the restaurant, distracted by the noise of a large group visible through the open patio doors…and faltered in her steps.

There were Nick and Jocelyn.

Terrah stared at him with his arm around her waist. Jocelyn was laughing and batting her eyes as they both chatted with the ad execs surrounding them, obviously having a great time.

"What's wrong?" Aidan asked as he turned his head to see what she was looking at. "Oh, I forgot to tell you the promotion luncheon was also going on here. We don't have to go over and say hi if you don't want to."

Terrah couldn't answer Aidan. She was too busy watching Jocelyn place a kiss on Nick's cheek. From where she was standing, it looked like Nick was enjoying every minute of the blonde's attention. Terrah's blood roared in her ears as she studied the two of them. Her rational mind considered the possibility that it was all a publicity stunt, but her irrational side was kicking up some major dust in her head.

Lying, womanising pretty bo –

"Terrah?"

Blinking, Terrah saw Aidan and the waiter patiently waiting for her to say something.

"Aidan! Come on over here."

"Damn, we've been spotted."

Terrah gave Aidan a weak smile. She knew he didn't really mind being the centre of attention again.

"This will only take a minute," Aidan told the waiter, not even bothering to ask if she minded walking over there with him.

She barely noticed his arm snaking around her waist as he propelled them both towards the crowd. Terrah forced her lips to curve upwards and said hello to faces she didn't even see as Aidan talked. She took a deep breath when his arm slipped off of her as he stepped away to autograph one of his photos. She turned her head and her gaze locked with Nick's. He didn't look happy to see her.

Her pulse quickened as he approached, despite the war going on in her head over what she'd just witnessed between him and Jocelyn. His manner was calm, but something in his eyes twisted her stomach into knots as he looked down at her.

"What are you doing here with Aidan?"

His dark tone annoyed her.

"Having lunch. Looks like you're enjoying your luncheon, too."

Terrah stepped back when Nick reached out to touch her. She looked away from the storm brewing in his beautiful eyes.

"This isn't what it looks like."

"Ditto."

"Terrah—"

She lifted her chin to look at his face just as Aidan rejoined them.

"You, my man, are a true professional." Aidan clapped Nick on the shoulder. "I couldn't have asked for a hotter photo shoot unless it had been X-rated."

Terrah didn't miss the flash of annoyance in Nick's gaze as he looked at the photographer. "I'm glad you got the shots you needed."

"Nick, they want to take a few more pictures with us," Jocelyn said, joining them with a girly giggle. "Can I snatch you away?"

For the second time, Terrah wished she'd got on the shuttle bus as she tuned out Nick's short response. She wished she were anywhere but where she stood.

Aidan turned to her. "Are you ready to go to our table now, Terrah?"

Terrah looked away from Nick's narrowed gaze as Aidan pressed his hand against her back again. She forced herself to nod eagerly at Aidan. "I thought you'd never ask."

"Goodbye, you two." Terrah flashed Nick a stellar smile. "Enjoy the rest of your meal."

"Thanks. You, too," Jocelyn replied with bubbly charm.

Terrah glanced at Nick. "Enjoy."

She didn't wait for his response, pivoting instead to follow their waiter, who'd been standing by patiently to take them to their table.

It was too bad her appetite had been completely ruined.

* * * *

Nick strode up the tiki-lit walkway towards Aidan's villa, forcing a smile as he passed familiar faces from the morning's photo shoot. He was pissed off. Every time he thought about Aidan's arm around Terrah he gritted his teeth. She was obviously under the wrong impression about Jocelyn. It annoyed him that Terrah could even jump to conclusions about him and Jocelyn after the afternoon the two of them had just spent together.

Having to turn down Jocelyn's invitation to go to tonight's party together had been even more irritating. She seemed hell-bent on seeing a connection between them because he'd slept with her. It had been pure torture for him spending the afternoon pretending to be into her, for the pictures the publicity and marketing team had set into motion for the promotional luncheon.

He usually didn't mind the PR gimmicks he had to do as part of a huge marketing campaign, but Jocelyn had taken it too far by kissing him in front of everyone. She'd left him with no choice but to return her kiss as their pictures were taken. Once the cameras had stopped flashing he'd expressed to her, in private, that he wasn't interested in dinner or anything else...period.

Needless to say, Jocelyn had not been pleased. No, she'd been livid, insisting they still had something they needed to discuss, but he'd walked away when Lyn had come over to talk. He'd left the luncheon shortly after.

Nick cursed under his breath.

The irony...

Jocelyn wanted him to respond to a connection she felt, which didn't exist between them, and Terrah refused to acknowledge the one he knew they shared. He realised the brevity of their time together, but there was no denying the power of their kismet-like chemistry after the way they'd been with each other yesterday. He knew Terrah felt it whenever they were together.

When he saw her tonight, he'd make her admit to it.

He still couldn't believe how cold she'd been at the restaurant. *Cold?* She'd been downright icy, talking to him as if they barely knew one another. If he hadn't known better, he would never have guessed she was capable of the fiery passion she possessed.

As soon as he'd got back to the hotel, he'd gone to Terrah's room and knocked on the door. When she hadn't answered, he'd sent her a text message telling her he wanted to see her, to which she'd replied, *See you at Aidan's party.*

Not exactly what he'd had in mind.

Exhausted, he'd showered and crashed for a couple of hours before getting up to dress for the luau. Aidan's party was the last place he wanted to be. He was burnt out on the social scene. Terrah was the only reason he was here. He wanted her back in his bed, moaning and calling his name like she'd been less than twenty-four hours before.

An image of Aidan's arm around Terrah's waist resurfaced in his mind.

Why had Terrah gone to lunch with him? Was she interested in the pompous photographer?

Aidan obviously enjoyed throwing lavish parties. Music was blasting and the night air was thick with the smell of barbecue. One of the female production hands from the shoot offered him a beer as he passed by, which he took with another tight grin.

Nick took a swallow of his beer, distractedly waving his hand to someone calling his name. Terrah was the first woman in a long while he couldn't wait to get next to again, and not just between the sheets. He liked the comfortable vibe between them. She was smart, sassy and fun to be around. He wanted to look her in the eyes, ask her about Aidan and tell her nothing was going on with him and Jocelyn…again. Once they cleared the air he could take her back to his suite and—

"There he is!"

A cheer arose from the partygoers when he stepped into the villa.

Party face on.

"Hey!" Nick called out as he caught the laurel leaf crown thrown in his direction. He pointed his finger at the guy who'd tossed it. "No props at a party."

Everyone in the room laughed as someone shouted out, "Let's worship the cologne god!"

Nick shook his head, waving off the few who'd actually lifted their hands up and down in deference to him. "I'm not wearing the cologne tonight, people, so I'm mortal like the rest of you guys."

A good-natured groan went around the room as Nick spotted Jocelyn. Her eyes narrowed as she stared at him for a moment. She was obviously still upset by their awkward conversation earlier. He considered going over to smooth her ruffled feathers, but there was a chance she'd take it the wrong way.

No, it was better he kept his distance. He didn't want to discuss whatever she wanted to talk to him about anyway.

Nick averted his gaze, scanned the room for Terrah and caught sight of her and Aidan through the sliding glass doors leading out to the deck and beach.

Shit.

Jealousy and anger warred within him as his gaze ran over Terrah's back. She looked deep in conversation with the photographer. He didn't give a damn if she'd come to the party with Aidan or not. She was going home with him. He crossed the threshold and stepped through the sliding glass door to join them on the deck. The sound of Terrah's laughter twisted something in his gut as he approached. He forced a smile onto his lips as he lifted his bottle to Aidan's beer salute.

"Nick, so glad you could join us tonight."

Us?

That one little word coming out of Aidan's mouth irritated the hell out of Nick as he shook the other man's hand.

"Hello, you two."

He glanced at Terrah, but she wasn't looking at him. She looked radiant and sexy, dressed in a flirty white halter top that drew attention to her honey-brown skin, and a burgundy ruffled skirt that highlighted the decadent curves of her hips and ass.

Finally, she turned to face him, sparking his blood as her gaze locked with his.

"Hey, Terrah."

"Hi, Nick."

Glossy lips barely curved up at him as she lifted her martini glass for a sip. Nick wanted to yank her away from Aidan, kiss her hard and stamp his claim on her.

Easy there, Slick.

He resisted, knowing he needed to act professional no matter how much he wanted to act upon the primeval urge.

"This is some party."

Aidan chuckled. "I've been known to thrown a mean shindig. Terrah can tell you."

The conspiratorial look the photographer gave Terrah seriously made Nick consider throwing all professionalism aside. He took another swig of beer, brushing off the red-hot flash of annoyance whistling through him as Terrah's posture stiffened.

"I always say, if you work hard, you should play even harder."

Nick half-heartedly laughed with Aidan, noticing that Terrah had straightened her hair. The dark strands brushed against her bare shoulders as she stared straight ahead. He wanted Aidan to leave so they could talk. Nick shifted his attention to the rowdy group partying on the other side of the deck.

"Well, it looks like you aren't alone in that sentiment."

Candles and tiki lights illuminated the scene, casting a warm glow over the festivities. More people were down on the beach, drinking around a brightly burning pit fire.

"Nick knows how to party, too. Don't you, Nick?" The look Terrah gave him was hotter than the lava flowing in Kilauea. "Aidan was just showing me pictures of you and Jocelyn at the luncheon on his phone."

She'd seen the kiss.

Good.

Well, it wasn't good, but at least she'd just shown him she gave a damn.

Laughter broke out and someone called the photographer's name down on the sand where a few had started to line dance.

"Oh, yeah, I always do the first line dance. You guys coming?"

Terrah waved her hand. "No. I don't line dance, remember?"

"Right. Well, I'll make sure the DJ plays something that'll get you moving out there." Aidan glanced in Nick's direction. "Enjoy yourself."

Aidan walked away from them, and another wild cheer arose as the photographer proceeded to dance to the front of the line. Nick turned away from the rambunctious scene, leant back against the railing of the deck and faced Terrah.

"I came to your room to talk after the luncheon."

Terrah watched the dancers below them goof off in the sand. "I went to the spa."

"Did you enjoy your session?"

"It was soothing."

She'd gone to take her mind off him. Pampering at a spa always made her feel better, but not today. Terrah had walked out of the salon feeling not the least bit relaxed afterwards.

"How was your lunch with Aidan?"

It was hard to meet Nick's steady gaze, but Terrah refused to look away.

"It was nice. Aidan likes to entertain."

She'd been bored to tears, but she wasn't going to admit it, especially after she'd seen that pic of him kissing Blondie. Her reaction to the picture had confirmed that, despite her best efforts, she'd invested more of herself emotionally than she wanted to admit in this fling with Nick. She had no one to blame for her heartache but herself.

Terrah shifted her gaze from Nick's, determined to keep cool. "Where's Jocelyn?"

"Who cares?"

She turned her face back to his with a bored sigh. "Apparently, your lips do."

"You're upset."

"No, I'm disappointed. Disappointed I believed your lines." Terrah looked up at Nick. "You got me into bed, so you can stop pretending there was ever anything else on your agenda concerning me."

"You're wrong."

Terrah scoffed. "Yeah, it was all a publicity stunt, right?"

"It was. The kiss was Jocelyn's doing. She surprised me with that and I had to hold up pretences for the sake of the pictures being taken."

"Did you fuck her for the sake of the job, too, Nick?"

Terrah regretted her words the instant she'd uttered them. She stared at Nick as her face heated up. The tension in his jaw was the only indication of his anger...that, and the glint of fury in his eyes.

"Nick—"

"You know what, Terrah? Forget it. Believe what you want about that kiss...about me. It's obvious I'm not going to be able to change your mind." Nick ran a hand through his hair. "I'm disappointed, too."

He turned and started to walk away from her before she could speak, and in that moment she believed every word he'd said.

Chapter Fourteen

"Nick, wait!"

He stopped in his tracks, came back to her, wariness evident on his handsome face.

"What is it, Terrah?" he asked, after seconds of silence had passed between them.

"I believe you about the kiss."

"Great."

The tension between them made her sad. She couldn't read anything from his schooled expression as he held her gaze.

"I'm sorry for what I just said about you and Jocelyn. That was in poor taste."

"This is all very polite, Terrah, but it doesn't tell me what I want to know."

"What do you want to know?"

"Do you think I've slept with Jocelyn since being here on the island?" Nick asked, studying her face.

"No, I don't. Did you come to the party with her?"

Annoyance flashed in Nick's eyes. "No, I did not. Did you come here with Aidan?"

"He offered to bring me."

"And?" Nick prompted as he stepped in front of her, effectively blocking her view of the people partying around them.

Her body reacted instantly to the heat swirling in the blue-green depths of his eyes. It wasn't fair—he looked like sex incarnate, wearing cut-off shorts with ragged holes on his thighs, a snug white T-shirt that hugged his biceps and stretched across his pecs.

"Terrah?"

She opened her mouth to say she'd come to the party alone when images of Nick's hard-on at the photo shoot flashed in her mind. Whether he'd slept with Jocelyn or not didn't change the fact that she needed to walk away. She knew from today she couldn't continue to indulge in a fling with him and not become even more emotionally involved.

"Let's share a final toast...to the success of today's *hot* shoot." Terrah twirled the guava martini in her glass and lifted it up.

"By hot, you mean my er—"

"Erection, yes."

"I see," Nick said, grabbing her arm.

"Hey, let go."

Nick didn't respond. He pulled her away from the deck railing and took them into the shadows. "Not before we finish clearing the air."

Terrah frowned as she glanced down at his hand on her elbow. "I didn't come here with Aidan."

"Good."

The rough pad of his thumb rubbed against her arm, causing goose bumps to emerge.

"Were you jealous about what you thought was going on between Jocelyn and me today?"

"Yes."

A warm breeze laced with the scent of barbecue fluttered through the tall, exotic plants shrouding them in the corner of the deck as they stared at one another.

Terrah exhaled, caught off guard by his bold question and her rapid response. Embarrassed, she tried wrenching her arm from his grasp, but he wouldn't release her.

"Damn it, Nick!"

She lifted her face to his and gasped when he yanked her close and crushed his lips to hers. He kissed her hard and, despite her chaotic emotions, she melted in his tight embrace. She wrapped her arms around his neck, giving in to passion with each dizzying, mind-melting caress of his tongue. Nick pressed her against the wood railing with his hard body and the loud music and chatter faded into nothing but background noise.

With considerable effort, Terrah broke the kiss and pushed him away. She glanced around the leafy potted plant to check if anyone had seen them and was relieved to find no one paying them any attention. Breathless she touched her tingling lips, furious at the triumphant gleam in Nick's eyes.

"I hope you enjoyed that kiss, because it was your last."

Nick laughed. "No. I don't think so."

Terrah took a few steps back from him. "I'm sure you don't, but I'm telling you it is. This has been fun, but—"

"That *display* everyone saw at the photo shoot wasn't for, or about, Jocelyn. I got hard thinking about you."

"What?"

Nick came to her, took her hand and pulled her back into their secluded spot. "You heard me." He snaked his arms around her waist. "I got hard in the middle of the shoot this morning thinking about *you*. I tried not to think about kissing you, holding you, but then you came over to fix Jocelyn's hair and my concentration was broken. All I could think about was how incredible it was being with you, and how much I wanted to be with you again."

His declaration melted her defences. She placed her hands on his chest as Nick closed the slim gap between them, making her very aware of his stiff cock. Her eyes widened as she looked up at him.

"*This*" — he pressed his hard-on against her — "is all for you."

Terrah suppressed a shiver of delight, hating the treacherous arc of desire snaking through her. "I can't do this."

"Why?"

"We spent one afternoon together. Let's just leave it at that."

Nick's arms tightened around her waist. "Your lips are saying one thing, but your eyes are saying another, Terrah."

She averted her gaze and Nick chuckled.

"I want you, Terrah. One day of pleasuring you is not nearly enough for me. Be honest with yourself and tell me it isn't for you, either."

Terrah's pulse raced from simply hearing the words 'pleasuring you' come out of Nick's mouth.

"Someone's going to see us together if you don't let me go."

"No one can see us over here, and I couldn't give a damn if they did. Tell me you don't still want me and I'll let you go." He ground his hips against her, making her crave him even more than she already did.

"Nick…"

"Wrong response. Let's try again. Tell me you haven't been thinking about how good I feel inside of you all day, and I'll let you go."

Terrah moaned with need and frustration. His words invoked the very mental image she'd been trying to compartmentalise in her head, to no avail. She was so wet. It seemed foolish and futile to fight against what she hungered for.

"I've been thinking about it. That's *all* I've been thinking about."

Terrah slowly exhaled as Nick dropped his arms from around her waist with a crooked grin.

"I'm glad I wasn't the only one. All day long, I was looking forward to spending more time with you...and not just in bed. Now tell me about Aidan. I know there's some history there."

Terrah nodded. "We dated before he was famous."

"He's still into you."

"I know, but I'm not interested in Aidan."

Nick responded by pulling her close. She closed her eyes as he claimed her lips in a slow, sensual kiss. Her core body temperature skyrocketed and her heart pounded against her ribcage. It felt so right in his arms. He caressed her back and Terrah moaned with delight. She knew in an instant the danger of falling for him was very real. She affected him just as much as he did her. Knowing that made it easier to accept the reckless emotions she felt for him.

"I want to take you away from this party," Nick said against her lips. "Do you want to stay?"

"I want to be with you."

"Do you have any idea what it does to me to hear you say that?"

She had a pretty good idea, if the way his gruff voice warmed every inch of her was any comparison to what he was feeling. More than anything, she wanted to ditch Aidan's party and be alone with Nick. He smelled so damn good and she wanted him naked...*now*.

Terrah lifted her chin to see his face as he stood back. The passion glimmering in his eyes sent a jolt of desire straight down to the wet heat between her thighs. She was slipping, falling headlong into something she knew had the potential to crush her heart, but she couldn't walk away.

"Let's get out of here."

"Okay."

Terrah followed him back out of the shadows of their secluded niche and back into the light of the tikis surrounding the deck. They reached the stairs leading to the beach just as Aidan bounded up them. He stopped mid-climb when he saw them.

"Hey! I was just coming to look for you, Terrah. Care to join me for a glass of wine by the pit fire?"

"I can't, Aidan, but thank you."

"I told Terrah I'd show her around the island."

"You guys are leaving my party?" The photographer's gaze shifted from Terrah's face to Nick's.

"We are. Thanks for inviting us."

Terrah could tell Aidan was annoyed as Nick gave the other man a wide smile.

Aidan nodded. "No problem. Have fun."

"Goodnight," Terrah said as he passed them on the stairs.

Terrah waited until he was out of earshot to shake her head. "You might as well have told him to back off."

"He needed to know sooner rather than later. He's wasting his time hitting on you."

"I can't believe you just did that."

"Why?"

"Word might get out that we left the party together."

"And?"

"Unlike you, I'm not used to being a gossip topic."

Terrah stared up at him as they reached the bottom of the stairs, captivated by the possessive light in his eyes. He might not care if anyone knew about them being together, but she did. Whatever was going on between them was likely going to end once they were off the island, and the last thing she wanted was her name thrown into the rumour mill. She'd worked too hard to build her reputation, which was just about everything in this business.

"Forget Aidan. He isn't going to say anything because he'd never want to admit the woman he wants isn't interested. He only likes telling stories that stroke his ego."

Terrah chuckled. "I suppose you're right."

They walked through the crowd of mingling bodies to the edge of the deck, and Terrah stopped when Nick paused.

"Do you want me to carry your shoes?"

"Are we going for a stroll on the beach?" She slipped out of her espadrilles and handed them to him.

"I promised to take you away from all of this" — he gestured to the wild group singing to the Eighties hit blasting from the outdoor speakers — "and I am a man of my word."

Terrah giggled as they stepped into the sand. They were a few feet away from the party when he took her hand and laced her fingers with his. They walked in the opposite direction of the luau, each step in the cool sand drawing them away from the noise and back to the natural tranquillity of the island.

"Look at the moon." Terrah stopped, spellbound by the luminous round orb and the moonlit reflection on the rolling waves. "It's so beautiful."

"Yes, it is. Being here makes you appreciate what you might not even notice in the city."

She nodded, falling into step with him once again. The balmy air felt good on her skin and being with Nick felt amazing. She glanced up at him in the moonlight and smiled as he turned and winked at her.

"Has anyone ever told you that you look gorgeous in the moonlight?"

Her breath caught in her throat as he squeezed her hand, lifted it to his lips and pressed a kiss against her wrist.

"What would you say if I said I was thinking the exact same thing?"

"I'd say it's another sign that we're in sync with one another. Connected in ways we don't even understand yet."

His words stunned her. "Do you really believe in that kind of thing?"

Nick shrugged. "I don't believe in coincidences. What about you? Do you believe things just happen...that people meet all by chance?"

"I don't know. One thing's for sure, it's all unpredictable." Terrah glanced at Nick as he started to chuckle. "What?" She grinned, pleased by the sound of his laughter. Then she knew *why* he was laughing. "Oh — my ringtone."

"I'll never be able to listen to that song and not think of you."

"Ditto."

Nick led them to a stone path obscured by lush plants and blossoms, which soon surrounded them as they continued forward.

"Oh, wow," Terrah said, pointing to illuminated bungalows now visible through foliage on the secluded beach. "Imagine watching the moon and sunrise staying in one of those. The view must be incredible."

"I'm sure it is."

Terrah frowned as Nick started walking towards the private beachfront properties spread out along the shoreline.

"I don't think we're supposed to be here."

Each bungalow was gated, surrounded by palm trees that guaranteed privacy.

"Come on, let's take a closer look."

"Nick! We're about to be trespassing," Terrah said when they stopped in front of a particularly lovely gated archway decorated with yellow plumeria flowers. This one was bigger than all the others they'd passed.

"Here we are," Nick said, producing a key from his pocket.

Terrah gasped when he unlocked the door and beckoned her inside.

"You've got to be kidding me! You upgraded your room to…to *this*?"

"I've always thought about staying in one of these when visiting the island. I wanted you to experience it with me."

He opened the door and Terrah stepped inside, gasping again in delighted wonder. The beach bungalow was a breathtaking space.

"Nick…this is incredible!"

Terrah moved forward, looking around. She shook her head in amazement. Her hotel room was plush, but the spacious and luxurious setting in front of her was magnificent. The living room was a picture of exotic elegance, the dark wood furniture complementing the light walls, and the Polynesian and floral accents. She could see the ocean through the huge, sliding glass doors leading out to a private lanai, where a sparkling pool was the focal point in a mirage of tropical plants.

"I can't believe you did this." She turned around to look at Nick, overwhelmed by the feelings surging up within her. "This is the most beautiful, romantic thing any man has ever done for me."

She went to him, rising on her tiptoes to kiss him. "I" – she kissed him again – "am swept away."

"Not yet."

Terrah squealed as he swept her up into his arms. She protested, laughing, as he carried her into the bedroom and placed her on the king-sized bed. Candles had already been lit, adding to the romantic flair already present in the lavish décor. She could hear the wind and surf through the open sliding doors that showcased the lit lanai.

"Champagne?" Nick asked as he popped the cork off the bottle.

"Yes, please." Terrah stood up, took the offered glass and held it up. "A toast…"

Nick smiled, lifting his glass to hers. "To?"

"Beautiful surprises."

"Perfect."

Their glasses clinked together and the sound of the fine crystal resonated in the room. Terrah took a sip, holding Nick's gaze as she swallowed the bubbly drink.

"Having you here with me has been all I've been thinking about all day, Terrah."

She didn't know what to say. His words and his smouldering stare sent a rush of heat over her skin that had nothing to do with her champagne.

"You really surprised me with this." Terrah gestured around them as she lifted her glass. "This is so good."

Could he tell how flustered she was?

Flustered? She was *aroused*, especially with him staring at her lips. Terrah squeezed her thighs together, conscious of the slick heat building between her panties and her wet flesh. Nick closed the small gap between them and desire unfurled deep within her. He took her glass from her hand and set it beside his on the table.

"Let me taste," Nick said, lifting her chin with his thumb.

Terrah's eyes fluttered closed as he kissed her. Their lips connected, moulding and melding into one. He pushed his fingers through her hair, and she let him guide her backward until they fell on the bed.

"I missed you all day."

His deep voice against her lips sent shivers of pleasure over her skin.

"Me, too. I was so upset to see you like that with Jocelyn."

Nick stroked her cheek. "I know, and I'm sorry, especially if you felt like I did seeing you with Aidan."

Terrah gave him a small smile. "Are you saying you were jealous?"

"Very."

"No need. I want you."

Nick pressed her into the soft comforter. He kissed her again, making Terrah moan with need when he pulled away.

"I missed touching you like this."

He kissed her neck, drawing his lips over her rapidly beating pulse point. He untied her halter top, exposing her strapless black bra as she arched her back. She opened her mouth to tell him it unfastened at the front, but his fingers were already there. Her bra fell open, Nick lowered his head to capture one nipple in his warm mouth and Terrah whimpered. His tongue drove her to pieces, alternating between long and short, wet strokes of magic.

She yanked on his hair. "Stop teasing and give me what I want."

Nick chuckled against her breast, then lifted his head to look at her. "And what do you want?"

Terrah arched her back as he tugged on her wet nipple.

"You. Naked. Now."

Chapter Fifteen

"I love a woman who knows what she wants," Nick said as he got up from the bed and tugged off his shirt.

She turned on her side, admiring the sight of his muscled arms and ripped abdomen. A rush of pure lust shot through her, emboldening her.

"Lose the shorts."

Nick slipped his hand into his pocket, tossed a condom on the bed and unbuttoned his cut-off shorts. With a small wink, he shoved them down over his hips, exposing his designer boxers and his massive hard-on. He slipped his thumbs under the waistband of his boxers and pushed them down to free his cock. Terrah's mouth went dry. She got up from the bed and the mounting wetness between her legs now soaked her thighs.

"Where do you think you're going?" Nick asked, his smouldering gaze running over her breasts. He watched her drop to her knees in front of him. "Ter — "

She took him in her mouth and leisurely suckled on the plump crown of his cock. Nick's ragged groan of pleasure spurred her on. She swirled her tongue around and around in teasing circles. The taste of his desire on her tongue heightened her own arousal. She gripped his hard ass and began taking him deeper and deeper between her lips.

"God, Terrah!"

She began to move her head, losing track of everything but the rhythm of pleasuring Nick. His fingers slid into her hair and he caressed her scalp as she concentrated only on the way he responded to her mouth. The more she stroked him, the more she wanted to feel him inside her.

"Woman" — Nick pushed her head back from his glistening cock — "you're killing me."

Breathless, Terrah licked her lips with a gasp when he yanked her to her feet and threw her back on the edge of bed. He grabbed her skirt and pulled it off to reveal her black panties.

"I thought I told you not to wear panties while we're together on this island."

"I'm sorry." Terrah lifted her hips, slid the damp fabric down and kicked the panties to the floor.

"Prove it. Show me what I've been thinking about all day long."

Nick dropped to his knees while Terrah slowly opened her thighs and parted her legs wide. Goose bumps scattered along her arms and what seemed like minutes rather than seconds ticked by, with Nick admiring her exposed pussy. He moved in close and she closed her eyes, anticipating the feel of his mouth on her.

"I love how wet you get for me." He whispered the seductive statement against her thigh as he cupped her mound.

Terrah inhaled sharply as two of Nick's fingers slipped inside her. She opened her mouth to say his name when his warm tongue darted over her clit and rendered her speechless. A tiny cry escaped from her lips when he began to feast on and finger-fuck her in earnest. She gripped the comforter and wriggled her hips in lustful abandon. He knew just how to tease her, adding the perfect balance of speed and depth to each thrust while flicking her clit with his tongue. Terrah couldn't control her moans of bliss, helpless to do anything other than fall over the cliff of ecstasy he'd taken her to. She cried out, and her voice covered the erotic sounds of him licking and stroking her as she came all over his fingers and tongue.

Nick lifted his head, giving her a satisfied grin as the last orgasmic tremor rippled over her. "You taste so good."

Trembling and breathless, Terrah opened her eyes when his fingers slipped from her quivering body. Nick grabbed the condom and she scooted back on the bed. Terrah watched him rip open the package and quickly don it. He was so hard and thick. She longed to take him in her mouth again, but that thought was forgotten as Nick moved up over her, between her legs, nudging the tip of his dick into her. He slowly filled her, his eyes never leaving her face, and Terrah's breath hitched in her throat. Nick covered her body with his own and began to move his hips.

Their gazes locked and she could see the control on his sweat-dampened face as he strove to pleasure her. Something in his eyes took everything she was experiencing to another level, moved her beyond the physical. Unexpectedly, tears filled her eyes and she bit back a sob as Nick stilled. She closed her eyes, overwhelmed by her emotions and the feel of his cock so deep within her.

"Are you okay?" Nick asked, brushing his finger over her eyebrow.

Terrah answered him with a kiss. She moaned with ecstasy through her tears as Nick picked up the pace, taking them both over the edge in a matter of minutes.

She wasn't okay. She was in danger of falling in love.

* * * *

Rays of sunlight, warm on her face, woke Terrah. She opened her eyes, rolled over in the warm sheets and reached for Nick. She groaned in disappointment to find him already out of bed. Slowly exhaling, she flipped onto her back and stared up at the ceiling. Long after he'd fallen asleep, she'd lain beside him, analysing her feelings where Nick was concerned, trying to find a way around the obvious. Nothing had changed in the morning light.

I'm falling for him.

Terrah placed her hands on her face, remembering his tender kiss after he'd asked her if she was okay. He'd seen her tears, but he hadn't asked her about them later when they'd shared a bottle of chardonnay in bed. They'd talked and laughed for hours before finally calling it a night.

How was she going to walk away from this sun-kissed fling with her heart intact?

After last night, Terrah knew her heart would never feel the same. His romantic surprise had melted away the last of whatever walls she'd put in place where he was concerned, and now everything seemed different—*felt* different.

Terrah reached for Nick's pillow and pulled it over her head with a low groan. The familiar scent of his cologne on the pillowcase filled her nose and her body instantly yearned for him. She shook her head beneath the fluffy down pillow.

Falling in love with Nick hadn't been the plan. She'd been willing to explore the attraction between them and enjoy a romantic fling, the first ever in her life, but now things seemed complicated. Shoving the pillow off her face, Terrah turned on her side and stared at the shimmering reflection of the sun on the lanai through the sliding doors.

Nick was a world-famous sex symbol. He could easily choose to love and be with some of the most beautiful women on the planet.

But he's here with me....making love to me.

That meant something.

But what?

Terrah sighed. No matter what his feelings were towards her, there was no denying what she was beginning to feel, not after last night. Not after the way he'd made love to her. She reached again for his pillow, brought it up to her nose and breathed in the subtle scent of his sexy cologne. A rush of heat raced over her body as she remembered the depth of passion reflected in his eyes as he had moved within her.

For as long as she lived, she'd never forget that look.

Nick paused in the doorway, his gaze running over Terrah's exposed back as she shifted beneath the sheets. It took a considerable amount of restraint not to walk over and get back into bed with her. He couldn't get enough of the way her soft skin smelt or tasted on his tongue, and he wanted to spend more time kissing her everywhere.

Later.

They had plenty of time. He was going to make sure of it.

Clearing his throat, he drew her attention away from the sliding glass doors. "Good morning."

She turned towards him, holding the sheet up over her breasts as she smiled. "Good morning."

The curve of her lips always had the same effect on him, warming him in places he'd never experienced before. She reminded him of a Nubian princess, effortlessly beautiful, lush and demure with her dark strands of hair brushing against the white sheet.

"I hope you're hungry."

"Starved."

"Good. I already ordered our breakfast. Do you want to eat by the pool?"

Nick stuffed his hand in the pocket of his shorts, noticing her gaze running over his bare chest.

Was she wishing he'd say 'to hell with breakfast' as much as he wanted to say it?

He was already envisioning ripping the sheet from her fingers and covering her body with his.

"Give me ten minutes?" Terrah said, just as he was about to move forward.

"Take your time. I'll be waiting for you."

Nick left the bedroom with a smile on his face. Terrah made him happy. He didn't want their time on the island to come to an end and he intended to make the most of every minute they had left together. Nick stepped into the living room and took a deep breath, enjoying the smell of the ocean. A gentle breeze swirled around the airy space and he started to whistle. He grabbed two flute glasses from the bar, feeling as carefree as the salty wind washing over him as he walked out on the lanai.

The scent of coffee, bacon and eggs wafted up to him as he approached their table. He bent down, careful not to bump his head into the white umbrella that blocked the sun. Gorgeous red flowers filled a glass vase in the centre of the tablecloth. Elegant dining ware showcased their omelettes and sweet rolls in delicious style. Sliced grapes, melon, mango and papaya filled a glass bowl, and there were carafes of orange juice and ice water.

Nick had just finished pouring them both mango mimosas when he felt his cell vibrating against his thigh. Reaching into his pocket, he took the phone out and lifted it to his ear.

"Hello?"

"Nick, it's Jocelyn."

Damn. He should have looked at the caller ID.

"What's up, Jocelyn?"

There was a pause on the other end of the line.

"I told you I needed to talk to you. I hoped we'd get a moment at the party last night."

"What is it? What do we need to talk about?"

There was a slight pause before Jocelyn sighed.

"I'm pregnant."

Irritation gave way to stunned disbelief as Nick frowned. "Excuse me?"

"That night we were together —"

"I used a condom."

He rubbed a hand through his hair as images from that night flashed in his mind. They had used protection and he was sure there hadn't been anything wrong with his rubber. He didn't know what game Jocelyn was playing, but he didn't believe her.

"Yes, you did, but—"

"Jocelyn, I know I'm not the only guy you've slept with in the last two months. We had sex. We used protection. There was nothing wrong with that condom."

"I'm telling you I'm pregnant and you could be the father."

"I don't think so. And you're telling me you're considering having this baby? What about your career?"

Jocelyn sighed again. "I don't know."

Nick cursed as he stared at the pool. This could not be happening.

"Jocelyn, I will need DNA proof."

"If I go through with this pregnancy, I won't do the test until after the baby is born."

"Understood, but we have nothing to talk about until the test confirms the baby's paternity."

"But—"

"DNA proof, Jocelyn." Nick gritted his teeth as he saw Terrah walking through the sliding doors of the bedroom. "Let me know if you decide to have the baby."

"Okay."

Nick ended the call as Terrah joined him, dressed in only his T-shirt. The white cotton stretched over her breasts and outlined her nipples with tantalising clarity. She stepped out of the shadow and into the sun, looking beautiful and concerned when she saw his face.

"I hope you don't mind. My clothes are a wrinkled mess."

Mind?

She was nuts if she thought he minded his shirt hugging her body the way he wanted to.

"I like this look."

He handed her the mimosa as Terrah stared at him.

"What's wrong?"

Every-fucking-thing.

He didn't want to tell her about Jocelyn's call. Sharing what he'd learned would effectively ruin the rest of their time together on the island.

Terrah placed her hand on his chest and took a sip from her glass. "You seem tense."

"I'm hungry. Did you enjoy your shower?"

"Those multiple shower jets are awesome! I could've stayed in there longer."

"You should have."

He pulled out her seat, brushed his lips against her temple and waited for her to sit down before taking his own seat. No matter what was going on in his head, he wanted Terrah to have a good time.

"Look at all of this food."

"You said you were starved."

"I am. You've depleted me of all my reserves."

Nick winked at her as they both helped themselves to the food. They ate their first couple of bites in companionable silence.

"This is so yummy. I could eat breakfast food for lunch and dinner."

"Me too. Did you sleep well?"

Terrah shrugged. "I slept all right. How about you?"

Nick thought she looked as distracted as he felt as she glanced up from her plate.

"I slept like a rock. Feeling your body next to mine all night long was effective as any sleep aid I've taken in the past. You wore me out."

Terrah cut her eyes at him, and he knew she thinking about all the erotic things they had done before finally drifting off.

He reached out to touch her hand. "I love sleeping next to you." He could feel her pulse speed up beneath his thumb as she stared at him.

"Me too—you're not a cover hog."

Nick laughed. "Thank you."

She squeezed his hand before pulling away to grab her drink.

"I think just about everyone is going back sometime today. My flight leaves around nine tonight—"

"Don't get on that plane."

Terrah's eyes widened. "What?"

She set her glass down as he ran his index finger over her cheek. "Stay with me. I've got two more days before I have to be back on the mainland and I want to spend them with you, here on the island."

He expected her to hesitate, but he was unprepared for the frisson of anxiety that zipped up his spine at the thought of her declining his invitation. They needed more time together. Something was happening between them and he was certain Terrah felt it too. If she left now, they might not get the chance to explore it any further.

Don't say no.

A flicker of excitement ran across her face before she frowned.

"Stay? I don't know… The ticket—"

"Don't worry about the ticket. Do you have another booking you need to be back for?"

"Not for a couple of days."

"Well, see, that's perfect. You're *supposed* to stay here with me. So…what do you say? Keep in mind that if you say no, I'll be forced to throw you in the pool."

Nick chuckled at the horrified look on her face.

"You wouldn't!"

"Nah, I wouldn't." He leant forward and kissed her softly on the lips. "But I do hope you'll say yes." He kissed her again, knowing he wasn't playing fair, but he wanted to make it harder for her to say no. "Come on, say yes, Terrah. I know you aren't ready to leave this place yet, either."

"You're right."

"So, you'll stay?"

"Yes." Her lips brushed his, and Nick could feel her smile before she moved back in her chair. "I'd love to stay."

"Woman, you've just brightened my day."

Terrah laughed, then frowned. "Brightened? Something *is* wrong."

"Nothing I can't handle." Nick patted his knee. "C'mon here."

He reached for her as she got up out of her chair, yanked her down on his lap, loving her girlish giggles.

"Are you ready to see more of this beautiful island?"

"Mmm…maybe later?"

She wrapped her arms around his neck and he kissed her. Her lips tasted like champagne, making him temporarily forget about the bomb Jocelyn had just laid at his feet.

For the next couple of days, he would concentrate solely on Terrah's pleasure. He wanted her to trust there was more between them than just great sex. She didn't know it yet, but he was determined to have her in his life for more than just a hot island fling.

Chapter Sixteen

Terrah sighed as she stretched out her legs. "This has been an incredible day."

"I'm glad I got to show you a little bit more of Hawaii."

"Me too."

They had spent the entire afternoon sightseeing and shopping, and Terrah had enjoyed every minute of her time with Nick. She hadn't laughed so much or felt so relaxed and happy in a long time. Terrah snuggled closer to him, resting her head against his arm, which was wrapped around her shoulders. Despite what he had said, she still got the sense something was bothering him, but whatever it was hadn't stopped him from showing her a good time.

"What did you enjoy the most? *Besides* shopping."

"Hey." Terrah playfully jabbed Nick in the ribs. "I didn't spend *that* much time shopping."

She placed her leg over his, comfortable in the oversized chaise. The soft rumbling sound of the water jets in the pool drew her attention away from the beautiful landscaping around the lanai and their beach bungalow.

"And I'm not complaining." Nick tugged on the strap of her new aqua-blue sundress. "I enjoyed watching you try on those clothes."

"I know you did, but I wasn't going to say shopping was the best part of the day."

"Really?"

"Nope."

Just being with you was.

"I really loved horseback riding along the beach. What a great suggestion."

Nick placed a kiss on her shoulder. "Mmm…that was nice. I'll tell you what was even better, though…"

"What was better than the horseback riding?"

She turned her face to look at him to see his devilish grin.

"Seeing you horseback riding in those jeans was the highlight of my day."

Terrah rolled her eyes, charmed by his compliment.

"Come on, Nick, you should've been enjoying the scenic view. Those waves were amazing."

"I was…I did, but all I kept thinking about was how beautiful you looked on that horse."

"Thank you. I'll never forget my first time horseback riding by the ocean."

"You're welcome, Terrah. I like surprising you."

Their gazes locked and her heart twisted in opposite directions. In an instant, the playful moment between them had become electric. She turned her body towards his and kissed him. He cupped the side of her face with his hand and Terrah sucked in a breath when Nick ended the kiss. She stared up at him and a whirlwind of emotion swelled within her.

"What are you thinking?" Nick asked, stroking her cheek.

"I'm thinking that the biggest surprise has been on me."

"What do you mean?"

There was no way she could tell him the truth.

"Terrah?"

"I mean—"

A noise along the fence distracted them. They turned to look and Terrah gasped at the sight of a telephoto lens pointed in their direction.

"What the hell?"

The fury in Nick's voice seemed to echo around the lanai as he shot up off the chaise. In a flutter of leaves, the lens disappeared from sight.

Nick was running toward the unseen intruder before Terrah could utter a word. Stunned, she stood up as he easily hoisted himself up and over the cement fence within seconds, leaving her to stare after him in shock.

Someone had just taken pictures of them kissing.

She wrapped her arms around her body. Minutes ticked by as she thought about what had just happened. She felt violated. Just the thought of someone capturing an intimate moment of her life on film without her knowledge was disturbing.

How long had that person been snapping photos? Thank goodness they hadn't gone any further than kissing.

"Terrah?"

She turned around to see Nick walking through the sliding doors of the bedroom with his cell phone at his ear. The terse words he uttered into the device barely registered as he approached.

"Are you all right?" he asked, setting his phone on the table.

Her gaze ran over his face. His handsome profile was a mask of controlled anger, a stark contrast to the warmth she had become accustomed to seeing. She felt the need to reassure him.

"I'm okay. I just can't believe that happened."

"Yeah." Nick ran a hand through his hair. "Neither can I."

"Did you see the person with the camera?"

"No, thank God for him. I don't know where he could've gone that quickly."

Terrah glanced over his shoulder as the doorbell rang. "That was fast."

Nick grabbed her hand, walked across the lanai through the sliding doors and headed towards the door.

"You informed the hotel already?"

"I called them while I was looking for that SOB."

Nick opened the door to reveal an attractive, ultra-tanned man wearing a suit.

"Good evening, Mr Tasso. I'm Rick Varga, the hotel manager." Rick offered his hand to each of them in turn as he shook his head. "First, let me apologise again for the invasion of your privacy. We take the comfort and security of our guests very seriously."

"How did this happen?"

Terrah glanced at Nick, seeing the tension in his body as Mr Varga rushed on.

"The hotel has been abuzz since news of your modelling shoot taking place here hit. We anticipated the press popping up, but, apparently, another guest staying in one of our private villas invited a member of the paparazzi onto the property without our knowledge."

Terrah sighed. "What about the photos the photographer took?"

"The photographer was not on the premises when we confronted the guest, who denied any knowledge of the photographer's intentions. She claims she didn't know he was a photographer and had only just met him at a party." Mr Varga cleared his throat. "She's apologised for what happened. I do hope this incident will not prevent you both from continuing your stay with us now or in the future. I would personally like to extend an invitation for the two of you to come back and stay here with us"—he gestured around them—"or in any of our other villas for a long weekend...free of charge."

The tentative smile the hotel manager gave them convinced Terrah he was willing to do just about anything to make them happy.

"Well." Nick widened his stance as he crossed his arms over his chest. "Mr Varga—"

"Rick, please call me Rick."

"Rick, that is a generous offer to consider, but I think right now both of us are more concerned about the photos captured."

"I understand, and, again, I do apologise on behalf of the hotel. We'll have extra security patrolling for the duration of your stay." Rick reached into his suit and extracted two cards, handing one to each of them. "We are still looking into this matter and, if I learn anything more, I'll contact you. Feel free to call me anytime to arrange a complimentary stay with us in the future."

"Thank you." Terrah shook Rick's extended hand and forced a smile onto her face as the man shook Nick's hand.

She went with them to the front door, her mind racing as the two men stepped outside. On edge, she walked back into the living room and switched on a lamp. She grabbed some matches, proceeded to light all the candles in the room, then stared at the flickering flames bouncing off the walls.

Who had taken the photos and when would they surface?

Terrah considered herself a realist, and she was under no illusions those photos would not turn up somewhere. Nick was a celebrity and those shots would be worth a lot of money for whomever had captured their kiss on film.

"Wine?"

She turned to see Nick with a glass of merlot in his outstretched hand. "Thank you." Terrah took the glass from his fingers and swirled the ruby contents around in the goblet. The liquid gleamed in the candlelight.

"You're worried."

She glanced up at Nick as he took a sip of his wine.

"I'm troubled." She stared at the wine moving in subtle circles in her glass, avoiding his eyes.

"I know. There's a chance the pictures will be leaked to the press."

"A *big* chance."

"And… What's your biggest concern? Terrah, look at me."

She lifted her face to his, touched by the warmth in his eyes.

"Are you concerned about our relationship going public?"

Relationship? Hearing the word filled her with joy.

"Is that what you're calling this?"

Nick's gaze narrowed. "What would you call it?"

Terrah shrugged, finally taking a sip of wine. "A fling?"

"A fling?" Nick repeated, before throwing back the contents of his glass.

Terrah nodded as he placed his snifter on the table beside them.

"You mean like a hot island tryst?"

His voice had dropped into that husky tone he used in the bedroom and Terrah's pulse quickened as she swallowed the semi-dry wine on her tongue.

"Yes. We're enjoying the island and each other."

Terrah lifted her head as he stepped into her personal space and grabbed her by the waist. She got lost in the aqua-green magic of his eyes as liquid heat replaced the blood coursing through her body.

"That's true, yes. We *are* enjoying the island and each other."

She gasped as his hands slipped over her hips to caress her ass. He palmed each cheek, bringing her closer to his body so she could feel his thickening erection.

"But, babe, this isn't a fling and you know it. A *fling* would imply that we both see and want an end to things between us in the foreseeable future."

"Okay, so what is it, then?" Terrah whispered as he gently squeezed her ass and guided her backwards.

He was so damn hard and she was so wet.

"The beginning of something I don't want to end. Tell me, Terrah, do you want this to end?" Nick asked as her back brushed against the wall.

It was an unfair question, especially with him touching her. She hesitated and he kissed her jaw before taking her lips in a soft, sensual kiss that left her wanting more.

"Do you, Terrah?" He took her glass and set it on the table. "Because I don't."

"Neither do I."

Her words elicited a growl of satisfaction from Nick. He pressed her harder into the wall and kissed her again. Terrah slipped her arms around his neck, intertwined her fingers into his thick hair and released a throaty moan. He caressed her tongue with his. Right now, here in his arms, she couldn't think about how long what they had would last. She could only concentrate on how badly her body craved his passion. It didn't seem to matter how many times they were together, she wanted more.

Concerns be damned. She hungrily kissed him back. His mouth slanted against hers and he slipped one of his hands under the hem of her sundress. She tugged on the dark strands of hair between her fingers as he skimmed his hand up her thigh to her hip. Terrah smiled against his lips when his questing fingers found her pantyless.

"You remembered."

"Yes."

His fingers skated over her hip and over the top of her pussy, teasing and warm.

"Touch me, Nick."

He obliged, making her whimper with need as he slipped his hand between her legs and dipped his fingers into her silky heat. Terrah widened her stance, wishing he'd pay more attention to her clit and make her come, but he continued to tease her.

"Please…"

"Please what? What do you want?"

She couldn't finish her sentence as he caressed her, forcing her to focus on the pleasure he was giving her and not the questions tumbling around in her head. Terrah struggled to shut off the rational part of her brain as Nick began to stroke her wet pussy in tandem with his tongue against hers. She writhed against the wall, ready for him to take her standing.

This kind of insatiable hunger was new to her. The depth of it shocked her. Neither of them wanted things to end, but she couldn't help thinking about what that meant, going forward.

Was she ready to risk her career—her reputation—if...*when* the pictures surfaced?

Terrah broke the kiss as her errant thoughts brought her back from the brink of passion. She unlocked her fingers from behind his neck, slipped her hands between them and placed them on his chest.

"What's wrong?"

"The pictures—" She shuddered as he pressed his palm against her clit.

"Forget the pictures. I'm mad as hell they were taken, but I don't care who sees them. I don't care who sees how I feel about you."

"It's not that simple."

She inhaled sharply as his fingers delved into her wetness.

"Isn't it?"

Wickedly distracted, she rubbed her hands over his erect nipples and smiled when his hand momentarily stilled on her wet flesh. Terrah looked at him through heavy eyelids. She moved her hands up over his broad shoulders and wrapped her fingers around his muscled biceps while he stroked her, fighting like hell against her arousal to get her point across. It was impossible to concentrate with him playing with her soaked pussy.

"T-the pictures will only add to your appeal...elevate your sex symbol status even further than one man deserves, but it could have the opposite effect for me and my career."

Nick's lips brushed across her forehead. "I'm sorry you are in this position."

The irony of his statement with his hand between her thighs made her smile. "No, you're not."

"I am. But are you trying to tell me you want to stop seeing me now, just because of the possibility of the pictures surfacing?" He slipped his fingers from her wet heat and used both hands to push the straps of her sundress off her shoulders, leaving her clad in only her bra. "Whether we continue this or end it now won't change anything if the pictures surface."

"So," Terrah pulled on his shirt and he yanked it off, exposing his sun-kissed abs, "the situation is hopeless?"

She feasted her eyes on his sculpted torso, all the way down to the waistband of his shorts.

"There's always hope," Nick said, giving her a sexy grin.

Terrah unbuttoned his shorts while he extracted a condom from his pocket and opened the package. She slid his shorts and underwear down over his hips, her attention drawn downward when he unrolled the condom over his engorged cock.

He led them to the oversized couch facing the lanai. She watched him lie down, her gaze drifting over the hard lines of his beautiful body to his dick, which jutted up between his long legs. Without a word, she straddled his thighs. Her knees sank slightly into the supple leather of the couch and she positioned herself over his dick.

"What are you hoping for, Nick?" Terrah teased, taking his hard length into her hand. She rubbed the crown of his cock against her wet flesh as he unhooked the front closure on her bra.

"All of you."

The searing look of desire in his eyes took her breath away. A throaty moan of delight escaped Terrah's lips when the head of his cock slipped inside of her. She slowly took him all the way in, enjoying Nick's ragged groan while he cupped her breasts and toyed with her nipples.

"Nick…"

Her voice trailed off and passion took over. She began subtly moving her hips, watching Nick's face in the flickering candlelight. He gripped her waist and she wanted to tell him he had all of her, everything she had to give, but words failed her. The sweet friction within her began to build. She placed her hands on his chest, giving in to pleasure, expressing her heart with her body.

Chapter Seventeen

After a leisurely shower and dinner, they ended up in bed. Classic songs from the Eighties serenaded them, along with the gentle pounding of the ocean waves they could hear through the opened sliding doors. The light from the pool and one candle remained the only sources of illumination in the room. Nick nuzzled the top of Terrah's head with his chin.

"Sleepy?"

"I don't want to even *think* about going home tomorrow."

"That makes two of us."

"Life is much less complicated on a tropical island."

Nick was inclined to agree, and he wrapped his arm around her back a little tighter. He wished they had nowhere else to go, no other responsibilities. As much as he was enjoying their extended stay, he couldn't fully put what Jocelyn had told him out of his mind. The model popped into his head every time he thought about how perfectly things were going between him and Terrah.

"Well, we could stay until my agent sends out a bounty hunter for me." He traced a line down the bridge of her nose as she shifted in his arms to face him with a smile.

"As tempting as that sounds, I've got a booking I can't change."

"And I have to fly out to Milan shortly after we get back."

Terrah shook her head. "I'm jealous."

"Don't be. I have to model suits during the hottest time of the year over there."

"How long will you be gone?" Terrah rubbed her palm against his five o'clock shadow.

"I think three or four days."

Nick twisted one of Terrah's thick curls around his finger.

Terrah sighed. "I've always wanted to go to Italy."

"You'd love it. The art, the culture, the architecture... It's a place that indulges all the senses." He intertwined his leg with hers, wishing he could take her with him on the shoot.

Parting from her for even a few days wasn't what he wanted.

"It sounds lovely."

She stopped stroking his beard and placed her hand over his heart. "Nick, how did you get into modelling?"

"Well, it started off as a dare."

"A dare?"

Nick nodded as he laid his head back against his pillow. "I wanted to contribute to my parent's efforts to pay for my tuition. Some of my college buddies posted an ad for a modelling agency on my door as a prank. I was nicknamed the 'pretty boy' of our group.

I used to hate it. I went to a casting call as a joke with my friends, but ended up being selected."

"And the rest as they say…"

"Is history, yup. I never finished college."

"What did you major in?"

He glanced down at, struck again by her natural beauty. "You'll never guess."

"Umm…law?"

"Nope."

"Medicine?"

He grinned. "No, although I *did* consider becoming a dentist."

"You, a dentist?" Tera chuckled as Nick shrugged.

"I had braces in high school and I was obsessed with having the perfect smile."

"You do."

"Ditto."

Terrah grinned. "So, tell me. I give up."

"I majored in English."

"Really?"

The incredulous look on her face amused him. He shook his head as she sat up in the bed, looking adorable as hell in the fluffy hotel robes they were wearing. "I used to quote poetry to the girls I was interested in."

"I hated English class, but if you'd been my teacher I would've definitely paid attention."

Nick laughed. "What about you? You told me a little bit about why you were drawn to makeup, but what's the full story?"

Her smile faded a little as she looked at him.

"Well, I didn't have a lot of friends in school. I was always the 'fat girl'." Terrah dropped her gaze as she tugged on the edge of her robe. "In high school, I was finally allowed to wear makeup and I loved the way it made me feel like a totally different person." She tucked a curl behind her ear. "I'd spend hours in front of the mirror trying different looks, learning what makeup worked best on my skin."

Nick turned on his side, reached out and touched her knee. He could see the pain in her eyes as she talked. It was hard to believe she'd been teased about her looks when he thought she was the sexiest woman he'd ever met.

"I started getting noticed for my makeup. Girls wanted me to show them how to apply it." Terrah looked down at her hands. "Makeup made me feel like I was accepted in the clique of girls in my school I wanted to be like."

"Why do I get the feeling something bad happened?"

"Something did. I overheard one of the girls I'd just showed how to use eyeshadow talking about my weight, calling me names. I ran all the way home in tears and I literally worked my ass off exercising over the summer."

Nick cursed. "Kids can be so damn cruel."

Terrah gave him a bright smile. "I started skipping meals, working out like a fiend. That summer, I lost enough pounds to no longer be considered the 'fat girl'."

"Did your family know about what you were going through?"

"My parents were thrilled to see me losing weight, but they had no idea what had jump-started my newfound determination. My sister did, though. College was better, my size was no longer an issue and I wasn't a social outcast. But it took me a long time to finally accept my curves and believe I was pretty, with or without makeup."

"You're gorgeous. I bet those chicks who teased you don't look half as good as you do right now."

Terrah laughed. "I used to dream I'd run into them now that I'm all grown up and professional."

"They would be jealous." Nick placed his arm over her waist as she lay back down.

"I'm over it now."

"Do you know how much I love your body?"

He leaned over and kissed her on the lips, wanting to bring back the sparkle in her eyes.

"I know you love these…" Terrah cupped her breasts through the terrycloth robe.

Nick pushed open the robe, bent his head and grazed one hardening nipple with his teeth. "I do *love* these, but that's not all I love."

"No?"

She giggled as he nipped at her earlobe, the sound of her sexy laughter making his cock stiffen.

"No. Woman, you've got *ample* delights and I've got a serious craving for them all."

"Sounds serious," Terrah said, giving him a mocking look of concern as she slid her hand past the opening of his robe and down over his chest.

"It is." He ground his teeth together as she slipped her hand lower, loosening the sash holding the robe together to reveal his thickening erection.

"Cravings can be bad," Terrah teased with a wicked grin, her fingers tightening around his cock. "Hard to resist, even…"

Nick shifted his body over hers, ready to show her just how hard it could be.

* * * *

The next morning after breakfast, Nick walked Terrah back to her hotel room.

"Are you sure you want to wait while I pack?" she asked, jostling two shopping bags in one hand to snag her key card from her purse.

"Absolutely." Nick took the key card from her hand. "I want to see how you're going to pack all this stuff back into that suitcase."

Terrah grinned. "I can do it—you'll see."

"Shall I get us some tropical mimosas?"

"Yes!"

They both laughed as he pushed open the door. Terrah set her bags down inside the room, giggling when Nick grabbed her. He pressed her against the doorframe and Terrah looked around the empty hallway.

"Nick! Let's at least close the do—"

He silenced her with a kiss that was both sweet and tempting.

"Sooo…the rumours are true."

Terrah and Nick both whipped around to see Jocelyn strutting towards them in a pair of pink, four-inch heels that drew attention to her black mini dress. She stopped in front of them and peered over her designer shades.

"Make-up artist shags hottie model."

"Watch it, Jocelyn."

The cool tone in Nick's voice was nothing compared to what Terrah was feeling as she leaned toward the female model.

"*Excuse me?*"

Nick held her tight when she made a move to step toward Jocelyn and it took every bit of Terrah's home training to bite back the nasty 'B' word that was on the tip of her tongue. She wanted to wipe the disgusted look off the model's face. It infuriated Terrah, the way Jocelyn was acting like her being with Nick was the most ridiculous thing she'd seen or heard.

"Have a safe trip back home, Jocelyn."

Nick's tone was as even as the polite smile he directed toward the bellhop coming up behind her with luggage in tow.

"I" — Jocelyn lifted her chin and pushed her shades back into place — "can't wait to get back on the mainland."

"I'm sure." Terrah was certain she'd heard an edge in Nick's usually warm voice.

Jocelyn's lips pursed together as her gaze shifted between them. "Um...can I talk to you in private for a moment?"

Terrah sensed the tension in Nick's body, even though he hadn't moved a muscle, and she shifted her gaze from Jocelyn's to his. "I'm going to go get started packing."

Nick nodded. "This will only take a minute."

"Okay." Terrah stepped out of her doorway. She glanced at Jocelyn with a forced, tight smile. "Aloha."

Terrah closed the door on Jocelyn's half-hearted wave.

She could tell Nick didn't want to be bothered with whatever Jocelyn wanted to talk to him about. Terrah stepped out of her sandals and wondered what it was the model wanted to discuss.

Scanning the room, Terrah was deciding what to pack first when she heard a light tap on her door. She walked over, opened it and smiled when she saw Nick. One look at his face told her he hadn't enjoyed his conversation with Jocelyn.

"Sorry about that."

Terrah shook her head as he entered her room. "Can we say 'awkward'?"

"I'm glad she saw us the way she did."

"Really?" Terrah noted the grim look in his eyes. "You don't look too happy."

"Jocelyn can be a bit much."

Terrah snorted. "A bit much? She was rude as hell. I bet you anything she told the bellhop about that kiss in the elevator. She's probably tweeted about it already."

Nick shrugged. "Let's forget about her. We've got five hours left to enjoy this tropical sun."

Terrah exhaled as he wrapped his arms around her, trying to ignore the niggling feeling that Nick wasn't sharing what was really on his mind.

"Just five hours left? The time just flew by."

"I know and, sadly, waiting for you to pack up all this stuff is probably going to suck up *four* of those five hours."

Terrah wrenched out of his arms with a mock indignant look. "Will not! You go get those mimosas and I'll show you how to fold and stuff all of this" — she waved at the shopping bags and clothing on the bed — "in less than an hour."

Nick scoffed. "Less than an hour?"

"Mm-hmm."

"Bet."

"What are we betting?"

"You naked, wearing only those new gold heels you just bought, while I—"

"Bad boy!" Terrah tapped him on his chest. "Trying to tempt me to lose on purpose."

Nick gave her a slow, sexy grin. "You can make a wager of your own."

"I will. If I succeed in packing in under an hour, you have to give me a full body massage."

"Oooh…this is *my* kind of bet. It's a deal."

Terrah laughed as he held out his hand and they shook on it.

"Okay." Nick glanced at his watch. "It's eleven thirty-two and the clock…starts now."

Terrah followed him to the door. "Go get those drinks, but don't take too long. I'm looking forward to my massage. Take my key card so you can get back in."

She winked at him as he took the card from her.

"Are you sure you want to win this bet?"

The wickedly sensual glint in his gaze made her pause for a split second.

"I don't like to lose."

Nick stared at her for a moment before nodding slowly. "I'll be back."

Terrah waited until he was out of the door to exhale with a wanton grin.

"To lose or not to lose… What's a girl to choose?"

She smiled as she headed towards the clothes on the bed, ready to impress Nick with her packing skills. Humming to herself, Terrah lifted her suitcase onto the comforter and started rolling her clothing and arranging each neatly tucked roll inside.

Twenty-four minutes later, she was just about done. Her large suitcase was locked and sitting by the front door. She still needed to pack her shoes, but there was no way the two new pairs she'd just bought were going to fit into her suitcase.

I'll have to carry them on the plane.

Her eyes drifted to the shopping bag still lying on the floor by the door. She walked over to the bag, picked it up and brought it over to the bed. Sitting it down, she took out the shoe box, opened it and admired the gold heels nestled inside. She needed to finish packing. When Nick got back she was going to prove him wrong.

Terrah imagined the shoes calling to her, beckoning for her to try them on one more time. Unable to resist, she wrapped her hand around the heels and took them out of the box. She slipped them onto her feet, stood up and sauntered over to the full-length mirror. The hemline of the yellow wrap dress she was wearing was a little shorter than she would normally wear, and her legs looked fantastic in the sexy three-inch heels.

To hell with winning the bet—she wanted Nick to see her in the shoes again. Decision made, Terrah pulled the sash on her dress and took it off. She turned to the side, checking out her body in the lemon-coloured bra and thong she was wearing. Her brown skin had taken on a warmer glow from the Hawaiian sun, and the bright yellow shade stood out. Terrah cupped her breasts in the demi-cut bra and imagined Nick's hands on her body.

She rubbed her hardening nipples through the soft fabric and moaned softly.

Nick would love seeing her dressed like this.

The sound of the key card sliding into the lock drew her attention away from the mirror. She turned her head to see him walk in, and her heart leapt in her chest as his gaze ran over her from head to toe. He placed the drinks on the side table by the door before casting a quick glance to the few articles of clothing left on the bed and the unpacked shoes on the floor. Terrah stood still as he studied her in predatory silence.

"You lose."

His gruff voice sent a shiver of anticipation down her spine as she slowly nodded.

"I know."

"Get over here."

Those three words made her wet. Terrah took her time coming to him, revelling in the hunger evident in his eyes. She kept her gaze on his face, swaying her hips with each step she took towards him in her new heels.

This time, she didn't mind losing.

Chapter Eighteen

Nick gritted his teeth. Terrah was killing him with her little seductive walk. Her breasts were practically spilling out of her lacy bra, begging to be played with. His eyes cut to the mirror behind her, and the reflection of her ample ass made him rock hard. She was delicious, and he wanted her even more than he had the first time they'd met.

Cravings are addictive. Terrah's teasing words rang in his ears.

Hell, he *was* addicted and he didn't want a cure.

"I can tell that you've been working hard."

Terrah nodded, her eyes on his. "Yes, but I still lost the bet."

She wanted him to take her. He could see it in her eyes.

"Turn around."

She obeyed, pivoting slowly enough for him to see her curves from every angle. He stopped her when she turned for a second time, so that her back was to him. After unhooking her bra, he came up close behind her and brought his hands up to cup her breasts. He toyed with the hard nipples, enjoying her low moan as he lightly tugged on the sensitive tips.

"I think you still deserve that massage."

Terrah answered by rubbing her rounded ass cheeks on his denim-covered cock. He didn't have to slip his hand into her panties to know she was already wet.

"I brought you something."

"Mmm…what is it?"

Nick pulled out the bottle of vanilla-scented massage oil in his back pocket. He popped open the lid, brought it to Terrah's nose and squeezed it slightly so she could smell the heady scent.

"Oh, that smells so good."

Nick kissed her neck, squeezing her tightly with one arm before releasing her. "Go lie down for me."

He waited for her to lie on her stomach, and his engorged cock twitched at the beautiful sight of her stretched out on the white sheets. She turned her face to him and watched him strip out of his T-shirt, jeans and underwear. He walked to her, loving the desire evident in her gaze, which ran over his body to settle on his bobbing erection. As much as he wanted to slip into her wet, tight heat, he was going to make them both wait.

He got on the bed and straddled her legs, resisting the urge to slide his fingers past her panties and into her pussy. Instead, he squeezed a generous dollop of the vanilla-scented oil onto her bare back and rubbed his hands over her skin. The oil seemed to shimmer as he worked it into her skin in gentle, circular strokes.

"You've got amazing hands, Nick."

Her soft compliment brought a smile to his lips.

"Thank you." Nick continued to massage her. "You've got gorgeous skin."

Her eyelids fluttered closed as she grinned. "Thank you."

Nick pushed his hands up along her spine, over her shoulder blades and back again. His gaze fell on the yellow thong showcasing her ass, tempting him with its lusciousness. He pulled the thong down, squirted more oil on the rounded cheeks and rubbed the shiny liquid around and in between her ass cheeks. Terrah stiffened as he glided his finger over her anus. He heard her breath hitch in her throat as he touched her tiny virgin hole drenched in oil.

"No—"

"Shh…"

He pushed one slick finger into her ass and Terrah gasped.

"Nick!"

He answered her by sliding his finger in even further, pushing it in and out in slow strokes as Terrah gripped the sheets in her fists.

Later he'd show her how good anal could be, but he couldn't wait another minute to sink into her. He pulled his finger out, moved off her legs and reached for the condom on the bedside table. After ripping the foil package with his teeth, he quickly sheathed himself.

"Turn over."

She obliged, pushing her thong down and off. "Are you going to fuck me now?"

Her voice was husky and seductive as she bent her knees to take off her heels.

"Leave the shoes on."

Terrah left the straps on the heels alone and fondled her breasts instead. "I want you so bad, I ache inside."

"I'm going take care of that right now."

He inhaled sharply as she reached out and touched his dick.

"I changed my mind."

"What?"

"Go back on your belly."

Terrah hesitated, her eyes falling to his cock. "You're not going to — "

"Trust me, Terrah."

She held his gaze for a split second longer before rolling over onto her stomach. Nick straddled her thighs on his knees and palmed her ass with both hands before guiding the tip of his dick into her wet pussy. Her bottom against his skin was divine, the feel of her tight, slippery sheath around his erection beyond words. He forced himself to slow down, giving Terrah slow, measured thrusts as he watched her grip the sheets beneath them. Her moans of bliss made him speed up as he smacked one of her juicy ass cheeks.

Terrah cried out, and Nick knew it was more from shock than pain as he slid his index finger in between her cheeks to her puckered hole. With his next stroke he breached her virgin ass again, pushed his finger in as far as it would go. He finger-fucked her in tandem with his cock, faster and deeper. Terrah's cries intensified and her body went rigid, then quivered around his cock and he knew she'd come. The sensation of her soaked walls milking his dick set off his own ripcord release.

Ripples of pleasure made him groan as he shuddered against her soft body. A bead of his sweat fell onto Terrah's back, and he rubbed it away after the last orgasmic aftershock unwound through him. He slipped from her body and pressed a kiss against her shoulder as he lay beside her, still breathing hard.

Terrah turned on her side, moving back so her body was nestled against his. She felt perfect in his arms as he placed his arm over hers, hugging her tightly.

He didn't ever want to let her go.

Tell her.

"I've been spoiled by the Hawaiian sun, and you." Terrah let out a tiny sigh as she stroked his arm. "I don't want to go back to the real world."

"I know."

Neither do I.

Especially after learning that Jocelyn was planning on keeping the baby that could possibly be his. The very thought of sharing a child with Jocelyn riddled him with anxiety.

Nick pulled Terrah closer to him and an image of *her* carrying his child popped into his mind. The idea did not make him uneasy.

The realisation of that thought confirmed what he already knew.

He had completely fallen for Terrah.

* * * *

Terrah placed her coffee mug on the kitchen counter, preparing to pour another cup as she absently listened to the television in the living room. It had been almost two weeks since she'd got back from Hawaii and she still didn't feel like she was back in the swing of things. Her work hadn't suffered, but she was distracted.

She was in love.

Terrah could no longer deny it to herself. The irrational emotion hadn't changed, no matter how many times she'd tried to psychoanalyse her feelings. She'd completely lost her heart to Nick, somewhere between the mango mimosas and having a little fun in the Hawaiian sun.

On top of coming to grips with that emotional doozy, she was still concerned about the photos of her kissing Nick turning up somewhere. Every day that passed gave her a false sense of hope that they'd never show up, even when she knew that was just wishful thinking. Somehow those photos were going to be made public. It was just a matter of time and it was not knowing when or how they'd be shared that bothered her the most.

Nick and the photos…those were the only two subjects she seemed to be thinking about. At the oddest moments, she'd recall the wonderful time she'd had in Hawaii with him, and it only took an uninterrupted minute before erotic images of the two of them together would replay in her mind.

She'd wondered how things would change between them when they got back, knowing how hurt she was going to be if all they'd shared had really been a fling. Nick had erased her fears, managing to call her from Milan at least briefly every day since they had returned from the island.

Terrah smiled with the mug at her lips as she thought about their late-night conversations on the phone. He was the only man she'd ever been with who could make her laugh about nothing, and she couldn't wait to see him. She missed him like crazy.

Heaven knew she *craved* him like crazy.

Every time she'd talked to him on the phone she'd been so close to saying 'I love you' right before they'd hung up, but had decided at the last second to wait and say it in person.

Bull. You're scared.

The grin on her face faded as she blew out a breath.

She *was* scared.

Saying 'I love you' was a big deal. She still thought about the first and only time she'd ever uttered the words—to a heartless boyfriend who had wanted her for sex more than anything else. At the time, she hadn't been able to see it, not even when her sister had told her she was dating a jerk.

Lesson learned.

She'd been careful with her heart and her body ever since, never mistaking sex for love or vice versa.

What would Nick do to her heart if he knew he held it in his hands?

Terrah bit her lip as she padded back into the living room, sat down on the couch and stared, without seeing, at the television screen. He cared about her. She knew that.

Would she mess things up between them by telling him how she really felt?

She'd pondered that question over and over in her mounting excitement to see him again. He would be back in New York tomorrow and they had dinner plans. She'd spent the evening shopping for the perfect dress to wow him with. The teal, strapless slip of silk she'd selected accentuated every single one of her curves. She couldn't wait for Nick to see her in it.

Yeah, and you can't wait for him to take it off you, either.

Terrah groaned out loud. She was so horny!

All she could think about was his hands all over her body. Her nipples tightened as she remembered the feel of him stroking her ass and pussy. She'd never come so hard in her life. He knew how to give her pleasure, better than any other lover had.

Terrah snapped out of her reverie as a picture of Nick flashed across the television screen. She sat up straight, her heart beating wildly as the picture of their kiss on the beautiful lanai was projected onto the backdrop, behind five females ready to gab about the invasion of her privacy.

"No..." Terrah breathed as she fumbled for the remote and turned up the volume.

'In entertainment news, Nick Tasso, the gorgeous new face for Desired cologne, apparently has a new girlfriend, Terrah Bryant, a talented makeup artist in the industry.'

'Isn't he gorgeous, ladies?'

'Mm-hmm...'

Frozen, Terrah blinked as the television audience agreed with the giggling female hosts. The image of the women on screen blurred as the gabfest continued.

'And he's dating a real woman. She's no carrot stick—this girl's got some curves.'

'Curves? That girl is thick.'

'She's not fat.'

'No, she isn't. I didn't say that. I said she's *thick*. Curvy thick.'

Terrah cringed as the sound of the television audience laughing filled her living room.

'Good for Nick. I keep telling you, ladies, guys like something to hold on to. This hottie just proves my poin—'

Terrah turned off the television, hurled the remote towards the other end of the couch and got up.

"Damn it!"

Marching back into the kitchen, she poured more coffee into her mug and reached for the Baileys on top of her fridge. She poured in an indulgent dollop of the liqueur and took a sip just as her phone began to ring.

With another muttered curse, Terrah reached for her cordless.

"Hello—?"

"Girl, do you know they were talking about you on—"

"I know, Audrey. Why aren't you at work?"

"I'm working from home today. God, I can't stand that show. I was only watching it because I was too lazy to find the remote and change the channel. Forget about all that… I can't believe that model said that."

"What model?"

"You didn't watch it all?"

"No. I couldn't stomach more than a few minutes."

Terrah took another sip of her laced coffee. The warm liquid felt like fire going down her tight throat.

"I know." Audrey paused. "Are you okay?"

"Just tell me what the model said. What was her name?"

"You know…the super fragile-looking blonde one."

"Jocelyn Tyler?"

"Yup. Those females posted a clip of her talking about the sexy shots from that photo shoot in Hawaii. Jocelyn said the chemistry between her and Nick Tasso translated so well in photos because of their mutual attraction."

Terrah squeezed the bridge of her nose and briefly closed her eyes. "Well, what she said wasn't true. She's just trying to drum up more publicity for her career. There was nothing going on between those two in Hawaii."

"Oh, I know, because there was something going on between the two of *you*. Those pics I just saw of the two of you together were hot, sis!"

"Stop it."

"They were."

"Well, I couldn't deny that something was going on if I wanted to, with those photos of us kissing no doubt circling the Internet by now."

"And why would you want to? Was that kiss as hot as it looked?"

"Audrey, this is my private life on display for all to see. I can't believe my curves are being discussed on daytime television."

"Try not to let it get to you. Besides, you were wearing the hell outta that dress."

Terrah scoffed.

"No, really, you looked amazing and you were photographed kissing Nick Tasso! Worse things could happen."

"I knew about the photos—"

"And you didn't tell me? I'm *still* waiting to hear all the juicy details about your trip to Hawaii."

"Audrey…"

Her sister sighed on the other end. "You always were the secretive one. Wait a second. They're talking about you guys again."

"Just turn it off, Audrey."

"Shh!"

Terrah sighed as she reached for the bottle of Baileys.

"Omigod!"

"What?" Terrah asked, slamming the bottle onto the counter.

A few seconds of silence passed.

"Audrey!"

"They were talking about Jocelyn and Nick."

"Okay, nothing new there."

"No, this is new."

"*What* is?"

"Keep in mind it's a rumour."

"Just tell me what they said!"

Audrey sighed. "It's been rumoured that Jocelyn's pregnant with Nick's child."

Terrah froze as her sister's words seeped into her brain.

Jocelyn pregnant with Nick's child?

Impossible. He would have told her.

"I don't believe it."

"It might not be true."

Terrah laughed. "I thought I'd prepared myself for seeing my picture plastered on television and having my weight offered up for table discussion, but this..."

"Is crazy," Audrey finished.

Terrah squeezed the phone.

It couldn't be true.

"Terrah?"

"I'm here."

"I know it's a lot to handle. Nick didn't say anything?"

"No."

"Well, they're always saying this and that star's pregnant when they're not. Don't jump to any conclusions just yet."

Terrah didn't answer, recalling how tense Nick had been at certain times on the island. She remembered Jocelyn wanting to talk to him about something and the strange vibe she'd felt between them at the time.

"Terrah, are you there?"

"I'm here."

"Don't freak out about this until you talk to him, okay?"

"Sure."

"That doesn't sound convincing, but I'll take it. Well, at least tell me his kiss — that one I just saw on my flat screen — was as erotic as it looked."

Terrah smiled against the phone, despite her mounting anxiety. "Sis, it *totally* was."

Audrey laughed. "There was no mistaking the chemistry between *you* and Nick when I saw that photo. So, are you guys officially dating?"

"We haven't put a term on our relationship."

"Relationship, eh? Well, that goes *way* past just dating. I didn't even hear you use that term with what's his name?"

"Never mind."

"With Nevermind. So, just how into Nick are you, big sister?"

"All the way, Audrey."

"Hold up! Are we talking *love* here?"

"I know, and after what you just told me..." Terrah sighed. "Audrey, what am I going to do?"

"Talk to Nick."

"Even if the pregnancy rumour is false, I don't know if I can deal with all that comes along with being involved with a person in the spotlight."

"There would be challenges you'd undoubtedly have to face, but you have to remember, people are going to say and think whatever they want about you. Remember what I used to tell you in high school?"

Terrah sighed with a slow grin. "Never let someone make you *feel* what they think about you. Good advice, but it wasn't easy then and it isn't easy now."

"I know."

"And what if Jocelyn is carrying his child?"

"Whether she is or isn't won't change how you feel about him, will it?"

"No."

"Then I think you should tell him how you really feel."

Terrah squeezed the phone in her hand. "Thank you for not riding me about whether I can love him after such a short time."

"Hey, I know you. You wouldn't say those three words lightly."

"Aud, I could be wrong... Wrong about him. Wrong about what I feel."

"Is your heart telling you that?"

Terrah thought about Nick's smile and slowly shook her head. "I don't think so."

"When do you see him again?"

"Tonight."

"Well, I'm sure Nick's going to tell you that rumour is a crock of poo. Now, tell me what you're going to wear. I know it's something fabulous!"

Terrah distractedly described her dress to her sister, wondering what Nick would say about the rumour. She couldn't wait to look him in the eyes and find out the truth. Surely, he would've told her if he had known about Jocelyn.

Tonight, she'd wanted to tell him she loved him, had been ready to trust her feelings—and him—one hundred per cent.

Was she about to discover she'd made a mistake in love again?

Chapter Nineteen

Nick walked up to Terrah's condo building and buzzed up to her apartment while wishing he could change the past twenty-four hours. He waited for her to answer, anxious to see and talk to her. Originally, they'd been supposed to meet at the restaurant, but, after the firestorm he'd witnessed in the media concerning him and Jocelyn, he'd told her he'd pick her up. The cat was out of the bag, and he'd been wrong not to tell Terrah himself when he'd had the chance. She knew about Jocelyn. He could hear it in her voice, even though she had said nothing about it on the phone to him. He'd half expected her to cancel their plans and tell him to go to hell.

"Hello?"

Her voice coming through the intercom made him smile.

"Terrah, it's Nick."

"Come on up."

Nick opened the door as it buzzed. He stepped inside the entryway, walked up to Terrah's door and knocked. The door swung open and Nick breathed in the familiar scent of her perfume as his gaze ran over her. She was stunning in a teal dress that complemented her body. Her hair was pulled up into an elegant French twist, and dangly gold earrings twinkled in the light as she closed the door behind him and lifted her face to his.

"Hello, Terrah."

"Hi."

"I've missed you."

She gave him a small smile. "How was your flight in?"

"Long."

Nick followed her into the living room, admiring the larger-than-life photos of famous black models on her brick-red, painted wall. Each photo showcased the exotic makeup on the model's face. Her loft was roomy and stylish, decorated with floor-length mirrors and with artsy knick-knacks in every corner.

"I love these," Nick said gesturing towards her artwork.

"Thanks. I admire the models and the incredible makeup in those shots. Do you want something to drink before we go to dinner?"

"No, thanks." Nick watched Terrah turn off one of the lamps by her dark leather couch. He'd expected her to ask him about Jocelyn the moment he'd seen her. "We need to talk about something before we go. I think you already know what I'm about to bring up."

Terrah sighed. "Just tell me the rumour isn't true, Nick. Tell me you're not the father of Jocelyn's baby."

The edge in her voice filled him with regret.

"Jocelyn is pregnant and there is a chance I'm the father."

"Wow." Terrah shook her head as he crossed the wood flooring to stand in front of her. "Unbelievable. How long have you known about this?"

"She told me in Hawaii."

Terrah stared up at him, and the disappointment in her brown eyes hurt his heart.

"I asked you more than once if something was wrong, and you didn't tell me."

"I didn't tell you because I don't know anything for sure, and because I knew it would ruin the rest of our stay. I knew you'd start second-guessing us."

"I wish you had told me, Nick."

"I know, and I'm sorry, Terrah." Nick scratched his chin, frustrated he'd hurt Terrah. "Would you have stayed in Hawaii with me if I had?"

He heard Terrah exhale as she shook her head.

"Probably not."

"And that would've been a mistake…a mistake on top of the one I made with Jocelyn."

"What are you talking about?"

"Terrah, we needed that time on the island together. I needed you to know that what I am feeling toward you is more than just physical attraction."

"So you withheld a secret like *this* from me? Is that how you're going to spin this?"

"Terrah, I'm crazy about you. I didn't want you to use this as an excuse to walk away from me."

"That wasn't fair."

"I know."

She looked beautiful as she glared at him…rightfully indignant and sexy as hell. He wanted to kiss her and make her remember how much they had between them before she possibly threw it all away.

"I knew something was bothering you. I just couldn't have fathomed the cause. It wasn't fair for you to invite me to stay in Hawaii… to romance me" — her voice hardened — "to make me feel—"

"What *do* you feel, Terrah?"

She averted her gaze from his as she wrapped her arms under her breasts.

"I don't know."

"Yes, you do."

Terrah met his eyes as she shrugged, overwhelmed by what he'd told her. "You don't get to come here, drop this little nugget of news on me and expect me to bare my soul to you right here and now."

"I know you're angry."

"I am." Terrah ran a hand over her straightened hair. "I don't know what you expect me to say, here."

"I just want you to be honest about what you feel."

Terrah sighed, lowering her eyes from his to the strong column of his neck. Even in the middle of an argument, she wanted him. He looked amazing in his dinner tux, so tall and gorgeous with his dark locks falling across his eyes.

"Terrah?"

She lifted her gaze to his. "I-I…was beginning to trust you…to trust us."

Nick took a step forward and wrapped his arms around her waist. "You *can* trust me, and how I feel about you."

His husky words pierced through her fears and doubts. She did believe him.

"And how do you feel, Nick?"

"Like I don't want to ever let you go."

He hugged her tightly as she rested her head on his chest and closed her eyes, with her cheek against his dinner jacket. "I know this thing with Jocelyn is complicated, but I want you to know that I want you in my life." Nick pulled back and took her face into his hands. "Do you understand why I didn't tell you about this?"

"I understand, but I'm not happy about it."

Terrah knew he wouldn't intentionally try to hurt her. There was no way he could look at her the way he did and not care for her. His hands slipped from her face, and Terrah averted her gaze from his.

"What will you do if the baby is yours?"

Nick exhaled. "If it is… I'll make sure I'm a part of the baby's life."

Terrah nodded, still unable to look at him. She'd expected him to say nothing less.

"This isn't how I imagined becoming a father."

"*If* you are."

"If I am."

She lifted her face to his as he glanced at her, and the stress of the situation was evident on his handsome face. Terrah forgot about her anger and disappointment. She slid her hands around his torso and hugged him. The scent of his cologne enraptured her as he held her close.

"So are you going to tell me now we can no longer see one another?" Nick asked as he looked down at her.

"No."

There was no way she could walk away from him at this point, and Terrah was willing to bet he knew it.

"Does this mean you forgive me for not sharing this with you?" Nick asked as he looked down at her.

"It means I'm ready to go to dinner."

"All right, then. Shall we?"

Terrah grabbed her purse off the bar counter. "Yes, we shall. As long as you understand this is the *last* time you'll ever keep a secret that affects us both from me."

Nick held her gaze as he spoke. "Understood."

"Good. Let's go."

She led the way to her front door with a myriad of emotions clouding her thoughts. Relationships were complicated enough without the extra drama she was going to have to deal with regarding Nick and Jocelyn's situation. As much as her heart wanted her not to, Terrah wondered if she'd made a mistake by not ending things with Nick.

* * * *

Terrah walked out of Barneys humming a love song with packages in both hands. She was happy. The past month had flown by, between work assignments and spending time with Nick. He'd been in the States for the past two weeks and they'd made the most of their time together. Most nights they hadn't even gone out, and Terrah hadn't minded. She simply enjoyed spending time with him, wherever they were.

Not even the media's focus on Jocelyn's pregnancy or Terrah's weight and involvement with Nick could bring down her mood. She'd stopped watching the news, avoided the talk shows and ignored the tabloid magazines in the grocery store. Her feelings towards Nick were real and, more than anything, Terrah wanted to tell him how she truly felt, but the timing always seemed off.

Terrah put on her shades and acknowledged to herself that timing had nothing to do with why she was holding back the 'L' word from Nick.

She was scared.

What if uttering those three little words changed everything between them?

Her cell rang and Terrah sighed. She shuffled her bags to reach into her purse and answer the call.

"Hello?"

"Hey, babe, it's me."

Terrah smiled as she always did when he called her. "Hey…I was just thinking about you." She waited for him to say his usual, 'What were you thinking?', but there was only silence. "Nick, what's wrong?"

"Jocelyn just called to tell me she miscarried."

Terrah stopped walking in the middle of Madison Avenue. "Oh, wow. How are you?"

"You know, I'm sorry for her. She put up a cool front, but I could tell she was upset. I didn't even know if the baby was mine, but…"

"But?" Terrah prompted when he fell silent.

Nick cursed. "I can't help feeling relieved and that makes me feel guilty as hell. I don't know what to do here."

The angst in his voice made her wish she were with him.

"You did what you were supposed to do, Nick, given the circumstances. Where are you?"

"Finishing up a shoot. I really can't talk much longer, but I wanted to let you know."

"Nick, it's okay to feel what you're feeling. I know you didn't want this to happen to Jocelyn."

"Yeah."

"Do you still want to keep our dinner plans for tonight?"

"Yes. I'll send a car for you at seven."

"Okay…and Nick?"

"Yes?"

I love you.

"I can't wait to see you."

"You, too, baby."

"Bye."

Terrah ended the call, surprised by the tears in her eyes. The inner turmoil she could hear in his voice bothered her. She was going to wrap her arms around him the moment she saw him and tell him she loved him.

Tonight, Nick would know he had all of her heart.

* * * *

"Did I tell you how gorgeous you look tonight?" Nick asked Terrah, loving the way her full lips curved into a sexy grin.

"Only about *twenty* times."

Soft light from the tapered candles on their table seemed to dance in her eyes. Nick's gaze drifted over her cleavage, displayed in a stunning red dress that was damn near daring him not to behave like a gentleman in public. Unable to resist touching her, Nick reached under the table and squeezed her thigh. He was rewarded with her sexy laugh as he continued to stroke her leg beneath the silky material of her dress, mesmerised by her beauty. His gaze slipped from her face to the graceful line of her neck, which was exposed, since her curly hair was tamed into a low side ponytail he couldn't wait to pull free.

"I'm glad you love my dress."

That's not all I love.

"That dress is designed to distract and enchant men."

"It's definitely working on you." Terrah tilted her face up to his with that teasing smile he adored.

Nick bent his head and kissed her. "Babe, I can't wait to show you just how well it's working."

Terrah placed her hand on top of his. "Mmm…I can't wait either, but it would be a shame not to finish our dessert, here." She looked at the huge aquarium in front of them. "I still can't believe you did all of this…setting up a special dinner in the hotel where we had our first kiss and sending the limo—very romantic."

"I wanted tonight to be as memorable for you as that night was for me."

"You've succeeded, but you should know that night was very memorable for me, too."

"Oh, yeah? Was it the kiss by the fish?"

Terrah giggled. "Yes." She paused for a moment. "I'm glad we're ending this day together after the news you got."

"Me, too."

He lifted her hand to his lips and kissed her wrist. The familiar, intoxicating scent of her perfume filled his nostrils, making him want her even more. It was important to him she knew how much he needed her in his life, too.

"I want to thank you for not giving up on us when you first found out about Jocelyn. I know you considered it."

"I'd spent too much time in the Hawaiian sun with you to just walk away."

Nick smiled. "Let's get dessert to go."

He wanted her all to himself…no interruptions, no distractions.

"To go? What about your suite here?"

"We're going somewhere else."

Terrah frowned. "Okay…"

"So we're going to get our dessert to go and then I'm going to whisk you away to a secret location."

"Oh, really?"

"Yes. Does that sound good?"

He nipped her wrist with his teeth as Terrah nodded with a grin.

"Let's get out of here, then."

Nick signalled James, their private waiter for the evening, who came over instantly.

"James, we've decided to take the dessert with us."

James smiled with a slight nod of his head. "Of course, Mr Tasso. I'll have it boxed and ready to go immediately. I've been informed that there are some members of the press milling around in the lobby, hoping to catch a glimpse of you two together."

Nick glanced at Terrah, who had stiffened in her chair. "Great."

"If you wish to avoid them, I can show you both out through another exit."

"Thanks, James."

Nick waited until James had taken their dessert and walked away from the table. "We'll get out of here without the press knowing."

"I hope so. We haven't given them any new photos to splash all over for a few weeks now."

He could see the tension in her body as she took her napkin off her lap and placed it on the table.

"I know how you feel about having those pictures of us in Hawaii used as the subject of discussion on that morning talk show."

Terrah gave him a bright smile that didn't reach her eyes. "Did I tell you I gave up morning talk shows?"

"No." Nick stroked his thumb over her pulse. "We can avoid the press right now, but there's no guarantee we'll be able to in the future. This thing with Jocelyn is going to break as big news again."

"I realise that. I just don't want to deal with it tonight if we can avoid it."

In the future...

The last three words of his sentence rattled in his head as she held his gaze.

He wanted a future with her, and hoped like hell she did with him. Terrah had all the qualities he could've ever hoped to find in one woman. He loved her caring spirit. He loved being around her. She was beautiful, smart and down-to-earth, plus the sexual chemistry between them was amazing. But, most of all, he loved how they could talk to one another. She wasn't awestruck by his job and she understood the modelling business and all that came along with it.

Later tonight, when they were finally alone, he'd tell her exactly how he felt about her.

"Ready to make a break for it?"

Terrah nodded with a wry grin as James approached their table with their coats, and two neatly wrapped boxes tied with purple ribbon.

"Is there anything else I can get either of you?"

Nick glanced at Terrah who shook her head. "No, I think we're good."

"Thank you, James. Please tell the chef the lobster... Everything was delicious," Terrah said as she stood up.

"Yes, send my compliments along as well."

James bowed slightly. "Will do. Just follow me and I'll get you guys out through the east exit. The limo should already be waiting."

"Perfect. Thanks, James."

"No problem."

Terrah slid her hand into Nick's as they followed the waiter through the dimly lit room, past a door labelled 'Hotel staff only' and into the hallway. James held the door open and they stepped outside. The night air was warm, carrying the sound of wailing sirens off into the distance.

"Here we are. Hmmm… The limo's not here yet," James said with a frown, and lifted his walkie-talkie to his mouth.

Nick turned to Terrah as James inquired about their limo. "Which dessert do you want to try first?"

Chapter Twenty

"Mmm…the crème brûlée."

Nick pretended to be shocked. "What? Not the devil's food cake?" He wrapped his arms around her as she laughed.

"I want to taste them both" — Terrah rose up on her tiptoes to whisper in his ear — "but not half as much as I want to taste you."

Her words ignited the flame of desire he'd been trying to keep tamped down all night. His cock stiffened as Terrah kissed his chin.

"I'm gonna hold you to that."

"I'm counting on it."

James cleared his throat and they both turned to face him. "I apologise for the wait, but the limo should be here in a couple of minutes. Do you two want to wait inside until it gets here?"

"We're good, unless you do?" Nick looked at Terrah.

"We can wait outside — it's a beautiful night."

James nodded. "All right, well, just knock on the door if you need me. I'll be close by. Have a good night, you two," he said, opening the door again.

"We will." Nick handed the waiter fifty dollars as James stepped back inside the hotel. "Goodnight."

"'Night."

The door closed and they were alone in the alley.

"Can you wrap me back in your arms?"

Nick grinned as he pulled her close. "Of course. I love having you in my arms. You feel so good, Terrah, and you smell delicious."

Terrah giggled as he breathed in the scent of her perfume. She wrapped her arms around his waist and laid her head on his chest.

"Likewi—"

"There they are!"

Nick cursed as two members of the paparazzi appeared around the corner of the building, illuminated in the headlights of the limo pulling up from the opposite direction. The two men rushed forward as he guided Terrah towards the approaching limo.

"Mr Tasso, have you spoken to Jocelyn since you learned of her miscarriage?"

"No comment." He barely glanced at the reporter asking the question as the limo came to a stop and the driver got out and opened the door for them.

How the hell had they found out about *that* already?

"Is it true you dumped the supermodel to pursue a relationship with Ms Bryant?"

Nick resisted the urge to snatch the guy's camera, knowing his reaction would be caught on film. He took hold of Terrah's arm. "Get in."

He helped Terrah into the back of the limo when another photographer snapped off a few photos. It took all of his control not to punch the guy upon seeing the anger in Terrah's eyes. He slid into the leather seat and cursed again as another flash from the photographer's camera momentarily blinded him.

"Perhaps Ms Bryant would like to com—"

Nick closed the door hard, effectively ending the barrage of questions coming his way. "Drive."

"You got it," the limo driver said, pulling off within seconds.

He waited until the partition was up between them and the driver before turning to Terrah.

"Are you all right?"

"I'm fine," Terrah said as the limo pulled into traffic. "I thought we'd escape that circus this evening." She took in a deep breath, still seeing bright spots from the camera flashes.

"I know, and I'm sorry."

She turned her face to his, noting the hard look in his eyes. "How are you? I know you wanted to deck that guy."

It was obvious he was just as frustrated as she was about what had happened. "I did. I didn't want you to have to deal with that crap tonight."

"It's not your fault, Nick." Terrah leant back into the soft leather seat and watched the lights of the city whiz by. "It comes with the territory. I couldn't believe they knew about Jocelyn already."

"Me either. I hope that little fiasco didn't ruin our evening."

"No way." She shifted her body closer to him as she met his eyes. "Tonight was incredible. Thank you."

"You're welcome. I love romancing you."

Her heart skipped a beat as his last sentence sank in. For a split second, she'd thought he was going to tell her he loved *her*. She pushed back her feelings of disappointment.

"I've got two more weeks here in New York before my next shoot in Alaska."

"Alaska?"

Nick laughed. "I know. This will be my first time going. It should be interesting...and cold. Want to come with?"

"No way. I couldn't, even if I wanted to."

"Well, before I freeze my ass, I'm free for the next two weeks. And I'm looking forward to it."

"And it's such a nice ass, too." Terrah returned his smile as he traced a circle across her knee. "That's terrific. You deserve the break." She glanced out of the window again as the limo began to slow down, cruising through New York's Upper East Side.

"Here we are," Nick said as the limo came to a complete stop.

"Here we are?" She looked at him incredulously before peering out of her window at the beautiful apartment building they had pulled up outside. "We aren't going to a party, are we?"

She didn't want to ruin whatever plans Nick had for them, but the last thing she wanted to do was socialise with a lot of people.

"It's a surprise."

Nick winked at her. She waited for him to join her, then took his arm as he led her under the green awning towards the doorman already opening the door for them.

"Nick, please tell me we aren't going to a party."

"We aren't going to a party."

They crossed the lobby to get to the elevator and Terrah breathed a sigh of relief. "Thank goodness."

Terrah could see their reflections in the gleaming steel of the elevator doors in front of them.

"I wouldn't dream of sharing you with anyone else tonight." Nick glanced at her. "I'm guessing you're feeling the same way?"

Terrah smiled and absently rubbed her temples. "Yes, I am."

"What's wrong?" Nick asked, observing her movements. "Your mood seems to have shifted since we left the restaurant."

"I've got a little headache coming — it's nothing."

Terrah slipped her hand into his. Her mood *had* changed. Maybe the reporters had got to her more than she wanted to admit to Nick, or herself. She felt on edge...tired...crampy.

Great.

PMS... You are PMS-ing.

The elevator doors opened and they stepped inside.

"Well, it's a good thing we left when we did."

Terrah agreed, observing Nick pushing the penthouse suite button. "Care to tell me why we're going up to the penthouse suite?"

"Not yet."

His sexy grin made her feel a little better. The elevator doors opened, they exited the lift and Terrah gave him a questioning look. She followed him forward and wondered what he was up to. There were only two doors in the entire hallway and he led them to the second one. Terrah smiled when he lifted her wrist to his lips and pressed a kiss onto her skin.

"Tonight, we are going to eat our dessert alone."

His devilish smile made her chuckle. He extracted a set of keys out of his dinner jacket pocket and her eyes widened when he slipped the key into the lock. He winked at her before opening the door and flipping on the light switch.

"Oh, wow," Terrah gasped. She stepped past Nick into the gorgeous, fully furnished suite, which was elegantly decorated with modern furniture and colours.

"Do you like it?"

"Like it?" She tore her gaze away from the amazing, panoramic view of the city to find Nick watching her. "I *love* it."

"Good. It's mine."

Her mild headache temporarily forgotten, Terrah's mouth fell open as Nick started to laugh.

"Are you kidding me?" She gestured around the luxurious space. "You *bought* a penthouse suite on the Upper East Side?"

"I've been considering buying property in New York for a while. Now seemed like a good time to buy."

Terrah wondered why, but held off asking the question as she slipped out of her heels and padded across the plush carpet to stand in front of the fireplace. "Well, you've made a sound investment in this place. It's absolutely gorgeous. Show me everything."

She followed Nick through the spacious suite as he showed her each room. There were two bathrooms and two bedrooms, along with a living room and dining room, all fully furnished.

"This place is huge, and the interior decorator hit all the right notes in each room," Terrah said as they walked into the kitchen. She admired the dark wood cabinetry with glass windows that allowed her to see the fine dining ware in place, just waiting for use.

"I know. The moment I saw this space I could see myself living here."

"Congratulations, Nick." Terrah walked back towards him as she ran her hand along the kitchen island's marble countertop. "I'm so happy for you."

She placed her arms around his waist, loving the feel of his strong arms wrapping around her as he pulled her close.

"Thanks. This place is great, but do you want to know what makes me really happy?"

"What?" Terrah whispered, her body warming instantly at the look in his eyes.

"You...*us*, together like this." He kissed her forehead as he hugged her.

"I feel the same way."

She melted in his warm embrace and groaned when he moved away.

"Why don't you make yourself comfortable on the couch and I'll bring over our desserts? Do you have something to take for your headache?"

"In my purse," Terrah said, moving through the open kitchen to the living room. "You wouldn't happen to have any chocolate ice cream here, would you?" She giggled when Nick came around the corner and looked at her with an amused grin.

"You want chocolate ice cream, crème brûlée *and* devil's food cake?"

Terrah shrugged. "I'm PMS-ing."

"PMS..." Nick lifted his head. "Oh, I gotcha. Well, I don't have any chocolate ice cream here, but I'll get some."

"No, it's no big deal."

Nick held up his hand. "Hey, if my babe wants chocolate ice cream, I'm going to get rocky road, double fudge *brownie* ice cream." He chuckled as Terrah laughed. "There's a minimart right down the street."

He disappeared back into the kitchen, only to return with bottled water tucked under his arm and two plates with their desserts on top. Nick set the plates on the coffee table before handing her the bottled water.

"Here you go."

"Thank you."

She took the water, grabbed her purse and took out her small vial of aspirin. "Seriously, I don't want the ice cream as much as I just want you to join me here" — she tapped the supple leather beside her — "on this couch."

"Are you sure?"

Terrah nodded, swallowing the pills as Nick took a napkin-wrapped fork and spoon from his back pocket and sat down. "Very."

She watched him dip the spoon through the glossy top of the crème brûlée. Terrah smiled, parting her lips for a taste as he brought the flatware to her mouth. "Mmm…it's even better than it looks."

"Wait…" Nick took the fork and sliced into the chocolate cake. "You have to taste this next, so you can tell me which one you truly love the best."

Terrah took the offered bite, savouring the chocolate on her tongue as she closed her eyes, lost in pure choco-bliss. She opened her eyes when she heard Nick laughing.

"I guess I've got my answer."

He handed her the plate with the chocolate cake and picked up the other dessert.

"It's sinfully good. Are you sure you don't want some? I'd be willing to give you another bite."

"Enjoy it." Nick grinned. "I'm getting more pleasure out of watching you lick chocolate off that fork."

Terrah sighed with delight and then smiled, savouring another taste of the cake. "Any other time, I'd have chosen the crème brûlée."

"Sure."

"I'm serious, but tonight… I'm afraid this baby is *all* mine."

Nick waved his spoon in her direction. "Funny, I was just thinking the same thing."

"You were? Well, here then," Terrah leaned over to offer him a bite, which Nick refused. The intensity of his stare sent a jolt of pure awareness through her that had nothing to do with the chocolate on her tongue.

"Not about the *cake*, silly…about you. I want you to stay here with me while I'm in New York."

His proposal both surprised and disappointed Terrah. She finished the last bite of the cake and placed her plate on the coffee table. It was the second time she'd thought he'd been about to declare his undying love.

Get a grip, girl.

"Terrah?"

She focused on his face, pushing her thoughts as far away as she could, and smiled. "Not necessary. I don't live that far from here."

"I don't care." Nick set his plate on the coffee table. "I don't want to waste a moment while I'm here in the city without you." He reached for her, pulling her back against his body as he wrapped his arms around her.

His tender declaration filled her with happiness. She'd intended on telling him how she felt earlier, but the more time she spent in his arms, the more she realised she wanted it all with Nick…the whole 'I love you' enchilada.

"So what do you say?" Nick placed a soft kiss against her temple. "We'll get to fall asleep and wake up together."

"Mmm...that sounds..." *Like something I could get used to.* "Wonderful."

"So say yes."

"Yes."

There was no other answer she could give him. She wanted to spend as much time as they could together, too. Apparently, she was a masochist for heartache.

"Do you want to watch a movie?" Nick asked as he reached for the remote.

"Something with some action."

She settled back into the hard, warm line of his body and rested her head on his chest.

Nick flashed a quick grin as he turned on the flat-screen television. "What? No romantic comedy? It's not my favourite genre, but I'd be willing to watch one with you."

"No way—you gave up your portion of the cake. Pick a flick with lots of stuff getting blown up."

Nick laughed. "Okay...you asked for it."

Yeah, I sure did.

She'd asked for it the moment she'd let herself entertain the possibility of anything more substantial with Nick, and now she'd fallen hard for him...past the point of no return. It was obvious to her that he cared about her and wanted her in his life, but he hadn't fallen in love with her. Only she had made the mistake of letting her feelings go so far.

Terrah blinked at the huge screen, then gave Nick the thumbs-up sign when he selected a Jason Statham film.

Why couldn't she just be content with the way things were between them right now? Everything was going great and, yet, she couldn't stop hoping for more.

Come on, Terrah, don't be needy.

What she *needed* was to know whether Nick saw any real longevity in their relationship, going into the future.

What she needed was a contingency plan for her heart.

And what good would that do you at this point?

None.

Nick wanted all of her for the upcoming weeks, and she would be his. She would forget about everything else and simply enjoy being with him, loving him even if he didn't love her back.

"Comfortable?" Nick asked as he shifted his body on the couch, so they could both put their feet up.

"Very."

Terrah took in a deep breath and inhaled the familiar scent of Nick's cologne. The screen lit up and her favourite action star took off running as something exploded in the background. She focused on the movie, needing a distraction from her chaotic thoughts.

Why had she allowed herself to fall in love with Nick?

Chapter Twenty-One

The sound of a dresser drawer closing woke Terrah up the next morning. She shifted beneath the warm sheets with a lazy stretch as Nick cursed.

"Is it morning already?"

"I'm sorry I woke you. I tried my best to close that damn drawer quietly."

Terrah opened her eyes to see Nick pulling off his sweaty T-shirt.

"It's okay. I need to get up anyway. What time is it?" She tried not to stare at his glistening abs as he kicked off his gym shoes.

"A little after nine. I wanted to get my workout in early. Did you sleep well?"

"Mm-hmm... I almost forgot I wasn't in my own bed."

Nick cast a glance at her. "That's a good thing. I like the way you look in mine."

Terrah ignored the somersaulting butterflies in her stomach as she grinned. "And I like waking up to the sight of you half-naked and sweaty."

"Yeah?" Nick asked, coming closer to the bed. "Would you like to join me in the shower?"

She smiled as he stroked the side of her cheek with his thumb. "Would you mind if I lay here a little bit longer instead?"

"Nope. You want me to turn on the television?"

"Yes. I look forward to the weekends at home when I can actually lie in bed and catch up on all my recorded shows."

The sound of a coffee commercial filled the bedroom after Nick had turned on the television. "Here you go." He handed her the remote and pointed to the screen. "I'll be out in five and then we can go get some of that."

"Coffee, yes!" Terrah lifted her face as he leant down to kiss her lips. "Take your time. I might change my mind and join you after all." She winked at him as she absently flipped through the television channels.

"Make my morning, babe—"

They both froze as a picture of the two of them, after dinner the night before, flashed on the screen.

"Was that…?" Terrah asked, blinking at the screen.

"Go back."

She flipped back to the previous channel and stared at the high-res photo of the two of them up against the limo they took after their romantic dinner. She flopped back down on her pillow, closing her eyes as she listened to the reporter.

'The sexy Nick Tasso has been reported to have bought a stunning penthouse apartment in Manhattan. He's been spotted several times with Terrah Bryant, a noted makeup artist in the modelling world, after breaking up with supermodel Jocelyn Tyler, who, sources confirm, suffered a miscarriage yesterday. There's been speculation as to whether Nick was the father.

'The fact that Nick's apparently dating a woman with real curves has rekindled the discussion in many circles on just what a healthy body image for women is, and which body type is the most attractive to the opposite sex.

'Terrah, it would seem, has always struggled with her weight. Here's a picture of her in high school—'

Terrah gasped, sitting up fast. She stared as old photographs of her, when she'd been at least thirty pounds heavier, were showcased for the world to see. "Oh, my God, I can't believe..." She barely noticed Nick walking over and turning off the television.

Heat rushed to her cheeks as she shook her head. All of the insecurities she'd fought so hard to shatter about her body seemed to swallow her whole. She blinked, wishing the old photos weren't etched in her mind. Anyone watching the news channel would see her personal struggle with her weight in the past.

What would Nick think of her now, knowing how big she used to be?

Tears filled her eyes as she dragged in a breath and glanced up at Nick. "Well, now you *really* understand why I didn't have any dates in high school."

"Terrah, I'm so sorry."

"Me, too."

She cleared her throat, willing the tears not to fall. She was not *that* girl anymore.

Overweight, unwanted, undesirable –

"Terrah, look at me."

Nick's deep voice pulled her out of her dark thoughts. She lifted her face to his, embarrassed by the single tear that slid down her cheek as he came to her side.

"Tell me what you're thinking."

He sat down next to her and took her hand in his. The concern in his eyes made even more tears fill her own.

Terrah shook her head, uncertain whether she could speak yet without falling apart.

"Don't let that stuff get to you. I thought you looked cute in those photos."

"Stop it."

Terrah waved her hand in the air as she got up from the bed and tucked the sheet around her body. She could take anything else but the polite platitudes, especially coming from Nick.

"Stop what?"

"Don't say that just to make me feel better, because it only makes me feel worse." She refused to look at him as she continued. "I was chunky back then. Hell, I was *fat*. I knew it, everyone around me knew it. So don't tell me I looked cute when we both know I looked terrible."

"You were overweight, yes, but I still think you were cute. You allowed the people in your life to make you believe you were completely unattractive, and that wasn't true."

"Wasn't it?"

"No."

Terrah finally looked at Nick. "Well, it doesn't matter now. I'm not that girl anymore and I will never be again."

A moment of silence passed between them.

"But the girl from the past is still a part of *you*, and from the way you're reacting to those old photos... It sounds like you haven't reconciled with that fact, no matter how you feel about your body now."

"The whole world probably saw those horrible pictures! I always hated them."

"Terrah, it doesn't matter who saw them. That's not who you are now. So, why do you care?"

Terrah furiously swiped at the tears sliding down her cheeks. "Because I do!"

"I know you do, but ask yourself why."

Angry and frustrated, Terrah clutched the sheet around her in a death grip. "I don't expect you to understand, Mr I've-Had-A-Perfect-Body-Since-I-Was-Born—and I don't appreciate you trying to psychoanalyse me."

The words came out harsher than she'd wanted, all her pent-up fury poured into every syllable. Her eyes widened as Nick stood up from the bed. His face was devoid of any emotion, but the tension in the air made her heart sink.

"You're right. I don't have a clue." He barely looked at her as he unstrapped his watch and threw it onto the bed. "I'm going to shower."

"Nick..." Terrah stretched out her hand, regretting the tone she'd used with him, and the insecurities that had surged up and made her act like a child. "I'm sorry."

Nick shook his head. "Don't worry about it."

Terrah watched him as he turned and exited the room. She closed her eyes and took a deep breath as she listened to the sound of the shower coming on.

What am I doing?

She was taking out her frustrations on Nick, which wasn't fair, even if he couldn't relate to what she'd dealt with. After all this time, she'd thought she'd buried all her issues about her self-image. She had finally got to a place within herself where she felt comfortable, desirable...even sexy in her own skin, and she'd slain a lot of personal demons to get there. Or, at least, she'd thought she had.

Terrah went to her purse on the dresser and took out a mini hair clip. She let the sheet wrapped around her naked body fall to the floor as she pulled all of her hair back into a sloppy French twist and clipped it. With a shaky breath, she walked towards the full-length mirror on the wall outside the entrance to the bathroom. Her gaze drifted from her face to her full breasts. She ran her hands down her waist and over her rounded hips. Her palm rested over her soft belly as she looked at her thick thighs.

Nick is right.

She still hadn't fully made peace with the past.

Terrah exhaled as she stared at the imperfections of her body...imperfections she'd learned to celebrate.

How could she let a little gossip and a few pictures throw all her hard-earned self-confidence out of the window?

I am not the awkward girl in that photo.

No, she was *all* woman... A woman with delicious curves. She *was* proud of her body, and she wasn't going to let anyone or anything make her question that pride again. Nick was right—why should she care what people thought of her past when it was the here and now that mattered the most?

Terrah stepped into the bathroom and took in a deep breath of the fragrant soap scenting the damp air. She padded across the floor to the shower door. Nick's back was to her and her gaze ran over his naked silhouette behind the steamed glass. She wrapped her fingers around the door handle and pulled it open.

"May I still join you?"

Nick dropped his head down, and droplets of water fell from his spiked hair onto his face as he looked at her. He gave her a slow smile, and some of the tension within her faded when he nodded.

"I was hoping you would."

Nick held out his soapy hand. Terrah took it and stepped into the shower. He closed the door behind her and their bodies touched, sending shivers of awareness through her. Beads of water hit and warmed her skin as she lifted her face to meet his eyes.

"I apologise again for snapping at you."

"Apology accepted." He gently tugged on her chin. "I'm sorry if I came across as insensitive."

Terrah rubbed her hands on his soap-slicked skin, placed a kiss on his chest and watched rivulets of water slide over hard muscle. "What you said is true. I just didn't want to acknowledge it. The craziness of the media, coupled with the flashbacks from my past, made me almost lose sight of who I am on the inside."

"*And* out." Nick leant down to kiss her lips. His hands skimmed up her waist to cup her breasts. "Don't you ever question how sexy you are to me."

He toyed with her hardening nipples and Terrah shuddered. "Nick…"

"I love every curvaceous inch of you. You feel so good in my arms, Terrah."

He brushed his palms over her breasts and teased the pebbled flesh. Terrah moaned and tasted droplets of water on her tongue. She looked up into his handsome face and was overwhelmed by the rush of emotions bombarding her heart. "I love being in your arms, Nick." She lifted up on her tiptoes and touched his lips with her own, loving the tenderness evident in the aqua-green depths of his eyes. "I love your kiss."

He responded to her statement by crushing her to his chest as his mouth claimed hers. Terrah welcomed his heated kiss, entwining her tongue with his beneath the warm streams of water that cascaded over them. Driven by passion, she slid her hand between their wet bodies. She wrapped her fingers around his lengthening erection and caressed the taut flesh.

"See how hard you make me, Terrah?" His voice was a low groan as he turned her around so her bottom was pressed against his stiff cock. "I want you so bad."

"Then have me…" She closed her eyes as his hands slipped down her back to cup her ass. "Take me, Nick…*please*, before I die of arousal." Her voice wavered and broke as he slid one finger between her ass cheeks.

"Can you hold on long enough for me to get a condom?"

The husky edge in his teasing voice made her smile as she shook her head.

"I want to feel *all* of you."

"Are you sure?"

Terrah turned her head to look at him. "Very. We should've had this conversation already, but I'm on the pill and I'm safe."

"Ditto" — Nick kissed her shoulder as Terrah grinned — "to the last thing you said." He skimmed his fingers over her hips. "Actually, I'm not sure how safe this will be. Once I feel you — *really* feel you, Terrah — I think I'm going to be done for."

"It would be a sweet end," Terrah teased as she braced both hands on the shower wall and pushed her bottom against Nick's hand. She moaned as two fingers delved into her pussy. He teased her with slow strokes, making her wetter and hungrier for him.

"I want more, Nick."

He slipped his fingers from her body. He grabbed her hip with one hand and guided his cock into her with the other.

"I want to give you everything you need."

Terrah cried out when he filled her, his words sending pleasure through her that matched the feel of him moving deep inside her. She shuddered against him and he groaned. He gripped her hips, digging his fingers into her, and stroked her slow and deep. The soft slap of their bodies colliding blended with the rhythmic patter of the water splashing from the shower, creating the perfect sensual soundtrack to their passion.

I love you.

Terrah bit her lip to keep from saying the three words inside her head as she moaned in ecstasy. She moved her hand between her slippery thighs, touched her clit with the smallest of caresses, and splinters of pleasure ricocheted through her. Nick thrust into her with an intensity that matched hers as she lost control. The depth of her orgasm sent tremors throughout her body. When she could finally breathe, she called out his name as he climaxed. Terrah's mouth fell open and she struggled to breathe beneath the shower of water falling on them. Her body quivered along with the subtle pulses of his cock deep inside her.

"You are delicious."

"Mmm…" She moaned as he pulled out, leaving her feeling strangely empty. She turned to face him, thinking he had never looked more devilishly handsome, with his dark hair all wet and spiked by the water. He smiled down at her as he rubbed her shoulders.

"Remind me to always get you to shower with me," Nick said, reaching for the shower gel.

Terrah laughed as she took the offered wash towel from his hand and began to soap up her body. "I can't do this every single time. Look at my hair." She stretched out one of the tightly wound curls that had escaped from her clip.

"What? I like it."

Nick rinsed the rich lather from his body and moved back so she could do the same.

"That's because it's *wet* and curly. Wait until you see it dry and poufy."

"How poufy?"

Terrah giggled as he turned off the shower and opened the shower door. "We're talking *major* bouffant."

Nick chuckled as he wrapped a fluffy white towel around her. "Now, that's something I'd like to see."

"I bet."

She threw her hair clip at him as he finished drying off with his towel and cinched it around his waist.

"Hey!"

He charged toward her, and Terrah screamed with delight as he chased her back into the bedroom. He caught her around the waist and tossed her onto the bed, laughing as hard as she was until his cell began to ring on the nightstand.

"I'm going to deal with you right after I take this call."

Terrah stuck out her tongue at him as he answered his phone. She scooted off the bed, pretending not to listen as she ditched her towel, rummaged and found one of Nick's T-shirts in his dresser. Apparently, his agent was on the other line, sharing some news about a big modelling offer. Terrah pulled the T-shirt on over her head with a little smile. She loved wearing Nick's clothes.

"You are not going to believe this," Nick said, placing his phone back on the nightstand as he looked at her.

"What?"

She loved seeing the excitement in his eyes as he came over to where she was standing.

"That was my agent. He just told me Rogue Jeans wants to use me in their next modelling campaign."

"Wow! That's incredible news, Nick — congratulations."

Rogue Jeans was one of the top labels in the country, and being chosen to represent their brand was a huge deal for any model.

"I know, right? I can't believe it — but there's more."

"Tell me."

"My agent told me they're promoting a new line for curvy women, and they'd like you to join me for this modelling shoot. They want *you* to model their new jeans."

Terrah blinked in surprise as Nick laughed. "Are you serious?" She couldn't hide her shock. The very idea of stepping in front of the camera made her extremely nervous.

"Very."

"That's crazy. I'm not a model."

Nick reached out and twirled one of her curls. "Well, they think you've got the look they need to sell this new line."

"For curvy women."

She tugged on his T-shirt as ad images for Rogue Jeans ran through her head. Models were usually shot wearing the jeans and little else, and all of them were about as far away from her body type as they could get.

Could she really commit to this?

"Yep." Nick's smile faded as he stared at her. "I take it you're not as thrilled as I am?"

Terrah sighed. "I don't know. I mean, honestly, the thought of stepping in front of the camera scares me."

"You'd be doing the shoot with me...and Jocelyn."

Chapter Twenty-Two

"Jocelyn!"

"I know. The marketing director for Rogue Jeans is convinced the three of us together will create the best stir for the ad campaign. It hasn't been confirmed yet whether she's going to do it or not."

"Count me out, for sure."

"Don't let her be the deciding factor, Terrah. Remember, they want you to showcase this line, not her." Nick cocked his head to the side. "Besides, if you're not there they'll pick someone else to pose beside me" — he dropped the towel cinched around his waist, and Terrah's eyes fell down over his muscled torso to his semi-erect cock — "and I only want *you* to do this with me."

"Ooh...you're really trying to distract me from the fact that I'd be in front of the camera...being compared beside Jocelyn. Or that I'd be agreeing to let my picture—"

"*Our* pictures."

"Our pictures be taken and shared in magazines across the world."

Nick stepped up to her and rubbed her shoulders. "The pictures would be fantastic. Think of how the publicity could benefit your work. You know the adage, 'There's no such thing as —'"

"Bad publicity... Yeah, I know, but I'm not so sure that's true."

"Well, you've got the rest of this week to think about it before my agent needs an answer. How does an omelette sound for breakfast?" Nick glanced at the clock on the nightstand. "Make that brunch."

"An omelette sounds good."

"Great. I'll chop the veggies if you crack the eggs."

Terrah grinned. "Deal."

"Do you need a pair of bottoms? I know you're once again lacking a change of clothes, although I prefer you dressed like that." He pointed at her legs and his T-shirt, which barely covered her nakedness.

"Give me some bottoms."

"And the lady decides to play it safe." He gave her a disappointed look as he opened his drawer and threw her a pair of soft cotton, drawstring pants. "I'll start setting up in the kitchen."

"Okay."

Terrah pulled on the pants in a daze as Nick exited the room. All she could think about was standing under those hot lights, trying to smile as she was asked to pose over and over again beside Nick and Jocelyn. It could be the ultimate opportunity professionally, and a major disaster personally.

At least she would be forced to face and conquer her demons once and for all by saying yes to the photo shoot, and truly showing the world what she'd been telling herself for years about her body. She was voluptuous and sexy and damn proud of every curve.

Terrah exhaled as she walked out of the bedroom and headed towards the kitchen.

Should she do it, or decide to play it safe once again?

* * * *

"Omigoodness, Rogue Jeans wants you to model their stuff! Are you freakin' kidding me?"

"No, I'm serious. Nick was chosen as their new model for the year and they asked his agent whether I'd be interested in modelling their new line, for us curvy girls."

"That's so cool, sis! I'm so happy for you!"

"Wait, there's more."

"More?"

"Jocelyn would be doing the shoot with us. They want to play on the hype of the three of us in the media."

"That should be interesting."

"And awkward. After everything that's happened I can't imagine how it would be to do a shoot with her and Nick. Audrey, I'm not sure I'm going to do this."

"What? I understand your reservations about doing this with Jocelyn, but this is an incredible opportunity and you'd rock the hell out of those jeans. I love those print ads. I can't believe you're even hesitating to do this. Do it and show that skinny heifer how jeans are supposed to be worn!"

Terrah giggled as she doodled on the magazine beneath her pen. "That's just it. Have you seen the chicks in those ads? They're half-naked and skinny as hell."

"And they don't want skinny, do they?"

"Yeah, but what if I have to get half-naked?"

"Look, don't obsess over the details. You should do this. I know you'll look amazing in whatever they want you to wear."

"Really? You're not just saying that because you're my sister?"

"Terrah, don't make me get on a plane so I can come over there and kick your butt. Of course I'm not just telling you that because I'm your sister. If your ass wouldn't look right in those jeans, I'd tell you. You'll look fabulous."

Terrah laughed. "Don't fly over here. It's just that… Well, you know I struggled with being self-conscious about my body."

"Yeah, I know, but that was in the past. Not now."

"I thought I'd put this behind me, but that stuff in the media did mess with my inner cheerleader."

"Rah, rah, rah!"

"I'm serious!"

"I know, I get it, I just couldn't resist."

Terrah smiled against the phone. "I know. Anyways, once I do this, everything about my body will be scrutinised and compared to Jocelyn's. You know it will be. I don't know if I can deal with that—my weight and body up for discussion by anybody and everybody."

"I understand. But, tell me the truth. Is there any part of you that wants to do this?"

Terrah thought about all those years she'd struggled with her self-image. She imagined herself doing the shoot, pulling it off and helping another young girl with the same inner battles to feel good about her body. In an instant, her answer became crystal clear.

She had to do this. Not just for herself, but for curvy girls everywhere.

"Terrah?"

"Yes! Yes, there is."

"Then you should totally do this."

"You're right, and you know what?"

"What?"

"I'm going to do it!"

Terrah squealed along with her sister on the other end of the line, the excitement of her decision and what she was about to do finally registering.

"I'm about to hang up with you and make the call with my decision."

"Good. I'm about to hang up the phone and book a ticket to the Big Apple."

"You're going to come here?"

"I know you don't think I'm going to miss this photo shoot with you and your gorgeous boyfriend. How is he, by the way?"

"Fine."

"Yes, he is! Besides that."

"Nick is great." Terrah chuckled as she stared at a picture of her and Nick on the fridge. The two of them had pretended to be tourists in New York, enjoying the sights and sounds of the city when he'd been in town for two weeks straight. "I can't remember the last time a man made me smile so much."

"Well, that's good, because you're going to need that smile for that photo shoot."

Butterflies fluttered in Terrah's stomach when she thought about what she was getting ready to agree to do.

"Yeah, you're right."

"Well, get off the phone and tell Nick you're going to do it."

"I am!"

"I promise I'll be there, so let me know the date."

"I will."

"I can't wait to see you. Don't forget to call me back when you have details. Love you."

"Love you back."

Terrah hung up the phone and dialled Nick's number with a huge grin on her face. He answered on the first ring.

"Hey, I miss you."

"We just spent two weeks together," she teased.

"It wasn't enough."

"Well, you'll get to spend some more time with me during our photo shoot together for Rogue Jeans."

"You're going to do it?"

"Yup! Your agent didn't say they changed their minds, did he?"

"No, they still want you—and so do I."

"Ditto." Terrah blushed as the husky timbre of his voice stirred her blood. She craved him, too. The onset of her monthly had prevented them from having sex the day after their hot interlude in the shower. She'd been more disappointed than Nick, who'd been unconcerned by it. He'd even pampered her with back massages and lots of chocolate treats. They hadn't been able to have sex for a week and it hadn't mattered, once again proving how perfect they were together in and out of the bedroom.

"I keep thinking of us together in the shower, remembering how wet and hot your pussy was around my bare cock."

"Nick!"

"Hey, I'm struggling here. I'm so hard for you."

"Don't tease me," Terrah moaned into the phone, imagining every delicious inch of his cock.

"I'm not joking. I need you…like right now."

"And I wish you could have me right now. How are things in Cali?"

"Rainy. All I can think about is getting into bed with you and whiling the hours away."

"Stop torturing me!"

"Are you wet?"

"Extremely."

"So, I could push my dick in with one thrust?"

"I said stop torturing me."

Nick chuckled. "Okay, I'll stop torturing you about how wet you are for me. I'll stop torturing you about how much you've been craving my cock."

"Nick!"

Terrah smiled against the phone as Nick laughed. God, she loved the sound of it.

"I'm going to tell my agent the news. He'll want to talk to you."

"Okay. Do you know when this shoot is going to happen?"

"I'm not sure of the exact date, but I'll find out later today. Terrah?"

"Hmm?"

"I'm really glad you decided to do this."

"Me, too."

"I can't wait to hold you in my arms again."

"And what else?"

"I'll show you in person in two days."

"Until later." Terrah laughed as she hung up the phone. She stared at the calendar on her fridge and sighed.

Two days was too long.

Her already damp panties became soaked as an image of Nick gripping her hips and taking her in the shower filled her head. The feel of his bare cock had been burned into her erotic memory bank. She couldn't wait to be with him again, and, when they were, she'd tell him 'no barriers'. She didn't want anything between them...not even those three little words. Whether he felt the same way about her no longer mattered.

No more barriers.

Not physically or emotionally.

She was finally ready to bare it all.

* * * *

Audrey clapped her hands as Terrah came out of the dressing room. "You look fabulous...just like I knew you would. And, see, you're not half-naked."

"I feel like it."

"You should wear your hair like that more often — it suits you."

"Mm-hmm... You know this isn't all my hair?"

Audrey reached out and touched Terrah's low, ultra-long ponytail, and the strands brushed along Terrah's waist. Terrah glanced down and tugged on the demi-cut scarlet bra she was wearing. She felt exposed, a tiny bit scandalous and a whole lot of sexy. Nick was going to love her outfit. Terrah admired the rhinestones sewn into the fabric, which sparkled beneath the lights in the hallway.

"The bra could have been a little bigger."

Audrey shook her head. "It's doing what it needs to do, trust me. The belt accentuates your small waist and those jeans... Girl, your ass looks amazing! I've just become Rogue Jeans' number one fan."

Terrah giggled. "I'm so glad you're here."

"I told you I wouldn't miss this."

Terrah hugged her sister as a rush of excitement and happiness soared through her.

"Have you seen Nick yet?"

Terrah shook her head. "No, not since we got here."

They hadn't had any time together in three days. He'd flown in from California late last night and they'd barely spoken to one another before they'd both been carted off for their wardrobe changes.

"What about Blondie?"

"I overheard someone complaining about her arriving late."

Audrey rolled her eyes as she fiddled with her phone. "There's a video of Nick fielding questions from reporters in California yesterday. Did you see it?"

Her sister turned up the volume on her cell and Terrah could hear Nick's voice.

"I try my best not to watch—"

"Shh! Listen, they asked about you." Audrey moved close to her, holding her phone up so they could both see Nick being bombarded with questions as he exited a building.

'Is it true you're doing a photo shoot with Terrah Bryant and Jocelyn Tyler for Rogue Jeans?'

'Yes, I am.'

Nick kept walking down the stairs and the reporters followed him.

'There's been speculation that you paid for Jocelyn to have an abortion. What can you tell us?'

Terrah stared at the video of Nick, seeing the flash of anger in his eyes as he coolly eyed the tabloid reporter who'd been brazen enough to ask the question.

'No comment.'

'Okay. What's your relationship status with Terrah Bryant?'

Nick flashed the sexy grin that always turned Terrah on. 'No comment.'

'Can we get your picture?'

Nick paused for a moment and a myriad of camera flashes popped in his face.

'What would you say to the people within the modelling industry who feel you're making a statement that could potentially hurt your career by dating a full-figured woman?'

Nick gave the reporter a wry grin.

'I'm not worried about my career.'

Terrah looked away from Audrey's phone as the video came to an end.

"I wished he'd said more there" — Audrey slipped the device back into her purse — "to make that reporter look like the dumbass he was for asking that question."

Terrah didn't respond. She wished he'd said more, too. He'd neither confirmed nor denied their relationship. She wanted to believe it was just for their privacy, but a part of her wondered if that was his only concern.

Maybe he was reluctant to say he was dating her for the very reason the reporter had suggested.

"Terrah? You've got that look on your face."

"What look?"

"The one that tells me you're upset."

"I'm fine. I've gotta go to makeup."

"Your makeup is already done."

Terrah gave her sister the 'Don't make me hurt you' look, which made Audrey laugh. "Look, I just need a moment before this whole thing gets started."

"I know. Go. I'll be in the studio, silently cheering you on when the photo shoot begins."

"Okay."

Terrah gave her sister a hug before walking away, determined not to let what Nick had said — or hadn't said—in the video she'd viewed bother her. She needed to concentrate on the shoot and that meant clearing her head. The last thing she wanted was for her disappointment to be captured on film.

Terrah exhaled as she walked toward the room where her belongings were, and paused when she saw Jocelyn with her back turned to her. The slim model was dressed similarly to Terrah, except her sparkly bra was green. She was digging into her bag, talking on the phone, completely unaware of Terrah's presence.

"I know. Of course, he doesn't want to admit he's dating her. Did you see those horrid photos of her?"

Anger surged within Terrah as she watched Jocelyn laugh and toss back her straight blonde tresses.

"I expected things to end when I had that photographer leak those photos of them in Hawaii—" Jocelyn turned around and her eyes widened as she saw Terrah. "Umm...I need to call you back," she said into the phone, before ending the call.

"*You*"—Terrah walked up to Jocelyn, who took a step back—"*you* were behind those photos in Hawaii?"

Chapter Twenty-Three

Jocelyn snorted. "I don't know what you heard —"

"Don't you try it!" Jocelyn flinched as Terrah wagged her finger at her. "I heard exactly what you said. What I don't understand is why you would waste time causing drama for Nick and me. Are you *that* jealous? Or is that you just can't deal with rejection?"

"Jealous?" Jocelyn gave a brittle laugh. "Oh, *please*. Nick may want to sleep with you, but that's *all* he wants you for. He won't even admit that you're his girlfriend."

Her caustic words cut deep as Terrah shook her head. "Were you even really pregnant, Jocelyn? I bet that was just a publicity stunt, too."

The model's face turned bright red. "How dare you?"

"What is going on in here?"

Both women turned to see Nick standing in the doorway, looking sexy as hell — shirtless, wearing only a pair of fitted Rogue Jeans. The tight, low-rise styled denim hugged and emphasised his sculpted torso, especially with his hands on his narrow hips. Terrah's eyes lifted from Nick's jeans to his face.

"I just overheard Jocelyn telling someone on the phone—*she* was behind those photos taken of us in Hawaii."

Nick's narrowed gaze shifted from Terrah's to Jocelyn's, and the scowl on his face only magnified the chiselled beauty of his face.

"Is that true, Jocelyn?" Nick asked, coming to stand beside Terrah.

"Terrah eavesdropped on my conversation." Jocelyn straightened her back. "End of story."

"I don't think it is, but it doesn't matter."

Terrah looked up at Nick as he wrapped his arm around her waist.

"Excuse me, guys…"

They all looked at the production assistant staring at them from the doorway.

"You're all needed on set. The photo shoot is about to begin."

"Great," Jocelyn said as she stormed past them.

Nick moved in front of Terrah as she lifted her face to his. Her brown eyes sparkled with anger as she shook her head.

"That female is unbelievable."

"Don't let Jocelyn mess this up for you."

He thought Terrah was gorgeous without much makeup, but now, with it artfully applied by another makeup artist, she was stunning in another way. Her beautifully expressive eyes had been highlighted with the perfect amounts of eyeliner and mascara, making the anger evident in their chocolate depths even more striking.

"I can't believe her. I can't—"

Nick bent his head and brushed his lips against Terrah's. "Forget about Jocelyn...the leaked photos...everything."

"I just saw a video of you with those reporters in California yesterday," Terrah said, moving away from him.

Nick shook his head. "Relentless."

The look on Terrah's face bothered him as she crossed her arms over her chest.

"What's wrong? Don't tell me you believe I paid Jocelyn to have an abortion."

Terrah averted her gaze from his. "No, I don't."

"Okay, good, but why do I get the feeling something is bothering you?"

"Why didn't you tell them we were dating when they asked?" Terrah asked, lifting her chin to meet his eyes.

"I never talk about my personal life in public."

"Is that the only reason?"

Nick frowned, not liking the doubtful tone in Terrah's voice. "What's going on in that pretty head of yours?"

"Since we've been dating, I haven't met a single one of your friends or family."

"Okay. I just met your sister today. We barely have enough time for one another and, when I do have time to be with you, I just want to be with *you*...no one else. I thought you felt the same way."

Nick ran the tip of his finger down Terrah's nose as she sighed.

"I do."

He could see she still wasn't satisfied with his answer. "Terrah, what did Jocelyn say to you to make you look at me like that?"

Nick watched her shrug, sensing more had been said between the two women than Terrah wanted to admit to him.

"Nothing. Forget it."

"No, I want to know. You don't think I'd have a problem telling the world you're mine?"

The tiny shrug she gave him made him want to whisk her off set and show her how wrong she was for thinking he had any problem staking his claim where she was concerned.

Terrah stepped forward and he took her back into his arms. "I don't care *who* knows how I feel about you." He took her lips again in a deeper, hungrier kiss. "Let's go take some of the hottest pictures this industry — *Jocelyn* — has ever seen."

They both grinned. The playful light in her eyes had returned.

"Now tell me, are you ready to do this with me?"

He cupped her chin in his hand as he held her gaze. His gaze swept over her naturally curly hair, which had been straightened, and he touched a strand lying across her chest.

"Yes."

"Good. I wish I didn't have to share you right now. You look so sexy. But I prefer your hair curly."

"You do?"

"Yes."

"That's good, because I can't deal with how long it takes to get this kind of hairstyle."

Nick frowned. "How long does it take to do a ponytail?"

Terrah laughed. "Don't ask."

"Can I take it down later?"

"You can try."

"I will."

He squeezed her hip with one hand and Terrah giggled as he laced his fingers with hers. They walked out of the room towards the studio and his gaze swept over her luscious body.

"Babe, you are wearing those jeans to perfection."

"Really?"

Terrah slid her hand from his and twirled around in her red heels for him.

"Oh, yeah. Show me your model walk."

Nick smiled as Terrah amplified the sway of her hips and walked in front of him. The curve of her rounded ass in the dark denim was something to see. He mentally talked himself out of a hard-on as he stared appreciatively at her small waist, showcased by the red belt around her naked torso. He was willing to bet her nipples were hard beneath the fabric of the beautifully beaded red bra that made her full breasts look even more tempting. Her outfit was designed to make a man conjure up a thousand and one lustful acts.

"Well?" Terrah turned to him as they reached the studio door. "What do you think of my walk?"

"I"—he placed his hands on her waist and yanked her forward—"think it's taking all my willpower not to drag you off this set, cart you off to my place and put you back in my bed."

"Are you going to be able to focus on the job?" Terrah teased.

"I guess there's only one way to find out." He took her hand and led them into the studio, where there was a flurry of activity going on. "Here we go."

"Oh, good..." Darien, the photographer for the shoot, zeroed in on them. "You're both finally here." He beckoned them over towards Jocelyn, who was already standing beneath the bright lights. "I want you"—he gestured to Terrah—"to stand in the middle with your arms crossed and your body slightly turned away from Nick, but look at him."

Nick watched Terrah follow his instructions and tried not to smile. He could tell she was nervous, but she was doing her best not to show it.

"That's it—now, Nick, you're on one knee in front of her. Jocelyn, put your hand on Nick's shoulder and lean in to him. Show how much you want him with your face. Great, are you guys ready?"

"No." Nick cleared his throat. "Not just yet."

A rush of excitement quickened his heartbeat as Darien nodded at him with a small smile.

"Nick, do you have something to say?"

"Indeed, I do."

Terrah noted the conspiratorial grin that passed between the two men before she looked down at Nick.

What the hell was going on?

Her heart began to pound as Nick reached up and took her hand.

"Terrah, I'm not waiting another minute...another *second* to tell you..."

"To tell me what, Nick?"

Her voice wobbled. She felt hot and shaky as her body reacted to the searing intensity of Nick's gaze, before he glanced down and stuck his other hand into his jeans pocket.

Blue-green eyes locked with hers.

"To tell you..."

Terrah couldn't breathe as he pulled out his hand.

"I love you."

"Oh, my God, Nick," Terrah gasped.

Tears filled her eyes as she stared at the exquisite diamond ring resting in the palm of his hand. She barely registered the camera flashes going off around them, Jocelyn's dark curse as she walked away while Nick lifted the ring up to her.

"I love you, Terrah. I want you in every way imaginable, and I want the world to know it."

"Nick...I... You... This is *crazy*!"

"Not half as crazy as I am about you."

Terrah tried to blink back tears, overwhelmed with joy. "I love you, too."

Nick flashed her the sexy smile that had captured her attention months ago. "Will you marry me, Terrah Bryant?"

"Yes!"

Terrah heard her sister squeal with delight in the background when Nick lifted her hand. She furiously blinked back tears in an effort to save her makeup as he slid the engagement ring onto her finger.

"There."

Nick swept her up into his arms and Terrah laughed.

"You are officially off limits," Nick whispered into her ear. More camera flashes went off around them. "I needed to do this before everyone on this planet sees how hot you are."

"It's beautiful," Terrah said, twisting her hand in the light. The diamond solitaire caught the bright lights in the studio and sparkled brilliantly.

"For a beautiful woman."

A tear managed to escape and slip down her cheek as the photographer cleared his throat.

"Uhh... I'm getting some great shots here, but do you two need a moment before we officially begin?"

"We don't need more time."

"We don't?" Nick asked, and Terrah shook her head.

"I'm ready. Let's do this." She looked from the glittering diamond to the man she loved.

Darien grinned. "Okay, but you do need a touch-up." He turned away from them. "Somebody get Jocelyn back in here, and Terrah needs makeup."

"Was Darien in on this?" Terrah asked, still stunned by the past five minutes.

"Yes. I'd talked to him about proposing to you before your run-in with Jocelyn. I'm glad I decided to do this here. I don't want you to think for a moment I'm not damn proud you're my woman." Nick brushed his thumb over her wet cheeks. "I want you to know that I think you look gorgeous, tear tracks and all."

Terrah grinned. "You're biased."

"Mmm...I don't think so."

He kissed her softly, with so much passion that Terrah's bones melted as his hunger for her translated through every fibre of her being.

"We need to get this photo shoot over with *now*," Nick said when he broke their kiss. "I want you to wear that bra and nothing else when we are finally alone."

Terrah lightly scratched her fingernails down his chest. "What's the rush? We've got ample time to be together."

Nick pressed his erection against her. "Yes, we do. And I've got *ample* delights in store for you later."

Terrah smiled. "Promise?"

"*I* am a man of my word," Nick said as he kissed the side of her neck.

"Yes, you are." Terrah exhaled in his arms, overjoyed and excited about her future. Their future together.

She was ready to model. Ready to see where love took her next.

About the Author

Nichelle Gregory has been in love with books and writing since middle school. A lover of the arts, she enjoys anything that embraces the creative nature within us all. Bringing believable characters to life that thrill and excite her readers is a challenge that continues to push Nichelle. She loves creating stories involving super sexy alpha heroes with divine heroines in magical, exotic, and fantastic scenarios. So, gone on…indulge your secret fetishes and desires!

Nichelle Gregory loves to hear from readers. You can find her contact information, website details and author profile page at http://www.total-e-bound.com.

Total-E-Bound Publishing

www.total-e-bound.com

Take a look at our exciting range of literagasmic™
erotic romance titles and discover pure quality
at Total-E-Bound.